Stealing Scarlett

LO GOLD

Stealing Scarlett © 2024 by LO Gold

This is a work of fiction. Names, characters, places and incidents are either the product of the authors imagination or are used fictitiously. Any resemblance to actual persons, living or dead, business establishments, events or places are entirely coincidental.

First Edition, 2024
Editing: Mara's Editorial
Proofreading: Mara's Editorial
Cover Design: Novel Hounds Designs

To all those readers out there who are looking for
a possessive, obsessive, and totally badass
woman with some serious female rage
— this one's for you.

PLAYLIST

AUTHOR'S NOTE

Dear Reader,

Thank you so much for reading my book. I hope you love it as much as I loved writing it! That being said, this is a dark book. Please do not turn to the next page if you do not enjoy dark and spicy books. This is a dark, paranormal romance–meaning that some things in this go beyond what's 'normal' for our world. There are demons, grim reapers, soul sharing, lucid dreaming, etc. This is also sapphic, meaning that the romance is between two women. If you don't like that then please don't read my book. It won't be for you and you should not continue reading.

This book contains mature content that is intended for a mature audience. There is a very long list of possibly triggering material so please make sure to read with caution. Triggering content includes but is not limited to: dubious consent, attempted sexual assault, domestic violence, murder, gore, talk of dismemberment, blood, suspended breath play, knife play, guns and knives used for threats of violence, violence against women, use of homophobic slurs, and more. If any of this isn't for you then please just close the book because I want all my readers to enjoy this book and not feel uncomfortable or triggered in any way. Your mental health matters! Please take care of yourself.

CHAPTER ONE

Morgan

I bounce up and down on his thin little cock as hard as I can. The likelihood of me getting off on this sad excuse for a dick is slim but a girl can hope, *right?* There was certainly no way I was going to get any kind of relief from him pushing his pencil dick in me gently, which is why I had no choice but to climb on top and attempt to take matters into my own hands.

"Oh yeah baby," he moans, his hands lightly holding my hips. "Just like that sweet girl."

That's the thing about most human men—they're always looking for a sweet little girl to take care of. They want someone warm and soft to snuggle with after they quickly get off. It's pathetic. This idiot is so desperate that he doesn't even realize that he hasn't found a sweet little girl.

No, he's been caught in a monster's web.

"You feel so good, daddy!" They also like to be praised, I've learned. They all have shockingly fragile egos.

"Yeah baby girl, you like daddy's cock tearing you apart?"

No.

"Oooo yeah, daddy! Please, don't stop!"

Not like you're doing any of the work anyway.

The man beneath me is pale and lean, with wire-rimmed glasses and a sad comb over. His lithe frame is nearly translucent and almost sickly beneath my beautifully tanned skin. It's like this dude just crawled out of the creepy basement where he lives. When I'd picked him on the Good Girls Looking for Dirty Daddies site, it was the glasses that got me. I couldn't believe someone was still wearing that shit. I thought as a society, humans decided that the creeper glasses from the 80's were no longer socially acceptable; that they screamed pervert. Apparently, my date missed the memo.

I guess his wife missed the memo too. I'm assuming he's married, based on the thin golden band on his left hand. Maybe he's separated. Honestly, who knows, and who cares.

We'd only exchanged a handful of messages before he found out I'm a curvy bombshell and asked to meet up that same night. In public, men pretend they want skinny bitches but behind closed doors, they all want a good girl with a body they can actually grab on to. His beady eyes haven't left my very full bust all night. With long blonde hair, captivating blue eyes, and curves for days, I'm what men are really looking to fuck. That's the beauty and the curse of my existence. I'm a beast from Hell wrapped in a beautifully seductive package.

Grinding my clit roughly against his pubic bone, I begin to feel my orgasm building. Tingles of pleasure build in my core and spread down my thighs. I moan sincerely this time as warmth begins to pulse through me, begging for a release.

"That's it, baby, let daddy make you feel good," the man croons as he palms a handful of tit and groans. His touch is light, gentle, sweet, and not anywhere close to satisfying.

"Yes daddy, I want you to make me come!" And I'm close, so close. No thanks to him, though.

The man's eyes roll back into his head, flailing upward, and exposing his slender throat to me. His Adam's apple bobs with each of his moans as warmth explodes inside me.

This motherfucker!

"Yes! Yes! Yes!" he screams in ecstasy while rope after rope of his sticky goop splatters my insides. "Take all daddy's cum, sweet girl!"

I know this little pencil dicked fuck did not just finish before I got to come!

I continue to grind, chasing my release, even after he stops throbbing inside me. His hands latch onto my hips as he tries to restrain my movements. His pencil dick begins to soften.

"Hey, hey. Stop, sweetheart," he says, laying a gentle

kiss against my heated skin. "You did such a good job. I came so hard. You can stop now." His tone is sickly sweet and condescending.

"What about me?"

"What *about* you?" His tone shifts drastically. Clearly, this human doesn't like being questioned.

"Don't I get to finish?" I ask with a cock of my head, letting him hang himself.

"You didn't?" He seems genuinely confused but I don't give a shit—I'm getting what I came for.

Releasing the barbs from my inner walls, I feel them slowly sink into his softening member. Razor sharp teeth that line the innermost recesses of my pussy bite into his flesh. I moan in ecstasy as his blood begins to seep out of him and into me. He screams as his eyes grow to the size of saucers as he feels the tiny teeth of my pussy ripping into his dick. Too bad it's too late for him.

"What the fuck?!" he shrieks as he squirms and writhes between my thick thighs.

"Shhh," I stroke the pasty skin of his paling cheeks. "Fighting it will only make this more painful and quicker," I begin to move my hips again, grinding against my horrified victim, "and I want this to last."

His blood drenches my insides and squelches with each thrust of my hips. I can see it seeping out from where we're connected, spilling across my clit, making everything warm and slick and fantastic. It's like self-warming lube…only red. I throw my head back and moan, relishing in the feeling of him bleeding out into me while simultaneously hardening again.

"That's it daddy, you're going to feed me all you got until there's nothing left!"

He's so pale. His breaths are coming out in short and choppy pants as I claim more and more of his soul through his measly little cock. But he can't stop the groans of pleasure from slipping past his lips as I coax him to come yet again, his essence steadily seeping out more and more. His soul is as measly as his little cock, but *fuck* the monster within me is relisheng in the agony etched across the man's face as my barbs sink deeper into him. Each roll of my hips brings me closer to completion.

"Yes," I moan in ecstasy. "I'm almost there, keep feeding me your blood and cum, daddy!"

I can feel my monstrous side coming out; my mask of beauty falling as I lose myself to the pleasure I'm pumping out of him. I don't even care if he sees the monster within, he won't be living to tell his tale anyway. Warmth builds and I can feel my release coming on fast now. My thick thighs quake around the pale and slender form beneath me as waves of euphoric release continuously build. The blackened veins of my Hellish form throb beneath the surface of my skin. Screams of agony and pleasure fill the small, shitty motel room. Red blood gushes down my thighs, filling the air with the scent of iron and sex.

As I fall off the cliff into ecstasy, I feel his life force slip from his body and into mine. Victim twelve is weak, but it should be enough to sustain me, for now at least. I'll need more soon. Thirteen before Halloween is the rule and we're already halfway through October. I'll have to hunt again soon.

CHAPTER TWO

Scarlett

Halloween has always been my favorite holiday. I love the brightly colored leaves that stick to the pavement and the crispness of a cool fall day. I love the excitement that permeates the air as children prepare to eat their body weight in sugar. I love the carved pumpkins glowing on porches and silkened cobwebs hanging across the front windows. I love the frights and fun, the tricks and the treats.

But my favorite thing about Halloween is that it's a day to be someone else. To be someone new. To dawn a mask and live a life different from my own. To wear the skin of a stranger, even if only for a night. On Halloween, I can be anyone I want. I can escape being *me*.

Don't get me wrong, my life isn't that bad. I have a

job I like, a good looking boyfriend, an adequate little apartment, and a cute as fuck cat. Life is generally pretty good. But on Halloween, I can be someone great. I can be bold, sexy, confident. I can be someone who I'm definitely not in real life.

I scan the rows of costumes in the giant warehouse Halloween store, hoping something calls to me. I'm not one of those girls who's smart enough to have a funny couple's costume planned out months in advance. I kind of just grab whatever calls to me. Currently, I'm drawn to a slutty Little Red Riding Hood costume. Its thick red cloak and short, little black corset dress would look vibrant against my pale skin and onyx hair. I'm not sure I have the curves to pull something like this off, though. I'm flat as a board and costumes like these are for beautiful girls with full curves. It'll probably make me look stupid and immature, like a little girl dressing up in mom's clothes. I can already hear Kyle's less-than-enthusiastic reaction to seeing me in something like this. Heat burns my cheeks at the thought. I shove it back into the rack with a sigh.

"Babe!" Kyle screams at me from across the store sounding excited. "Look at this one!"

Kyle and I have been together for about six years now. I moved to this town after high school and quickly found a job, hoping to save up enough to one day go to the local college. I grew up in some middle-of-nowhere town with parents who were born there and will die there. I did whatever I could to get out. As soon as I graduated high school I ran to freedom, I ran to the sea.

I ended up in this small Washington town, living in a small apartment, and working at a quaint little coffee shop. It wasn't the bold and glamorous life I dreamed of having when I left home, but at least I was free. One day, Kyle came into the coffee shop. He was older, a college boy, with the kind of looks that would bring most girls to their knees. I couldn't fathom what a boy like him would see in a girl like me. He was so charming. I fell for him instantly. He may not always be the best boyfriend, but we've started to build a life together. He's comfortable, stable, and usually pretty nice.

Six years later and I'm still working at the coffee shop; hoping that one day soon Kyle will decide I'm finally ready to start college. I've been studying on nights when he goes out, looking through college prep books, to try to prove to him it won't be a waste of our savings for me to finally attend classes.

Rounding several rows of colorful costumes, I spot Kyle holding up one in front of him with a huge grin struck across his handsome facade. He styled his blonde hair back out of his face today, allowing his beautiful eyes to shine. It was originally his eyes that drew me to him. They're almost gray, like the color of afternoon storm clouds. They remind me of the small Midwest town I grew up in, comforting me with a sense of home that I haven't been able to shake in all the years we've been together.

"What is it?" I ask him, assessing the long, white, two-piece outfit adorned with feathers.

His gaze shifts to me and I swear I see a flicker of annoyance cross his face. It's always this way in our dynamic—I'm the stupid, small-town girl who works at a coffee shop while he's the well-off college graduate. I'm meek and he's strong. I'm boring and he's fun. He says I'm enough for him, but I sometimes get the feeling that I'll never be quite good enough for him. Maybe once I have a college degree and a fancy job he will respect me more and will finally propose. We could be happy…I think.

"A pimp, obviously," his tone is bitter as he assesses me. His eyes flick back to the costume in his hand and a satisfied smirk pulls across his face. "It even comes with a big ass pimp cup! Think the downtown bars will be willing to put my drinks in this sick-ass chalice all night?" He holds up the clear plastic bag containing a golden cup and strings of golden chains. "It doesn't really go with the Heaven and Hell theme that The Jager is doing but I'm not sure I'm sold on the silent rave idea anyway."

"You really want to go to the downtown bars again? I thought maybe we could just relax this Halloween. You know, stay home, pass out candy, watch scary movies?" I hate going out to the bars with Kyle. He's always rowdy and flirtatious when he drinks. I know he always goes home with me, but that doesn't make it sting less when I have to watch him flirt and dance with other girls. He usually picks blonde, curvy, seductive women. The complete opposite of me. When we make it home and he closes his eyes to fuck me, I'm always worried he's picturing someone else.

"Then what the fuck are we costume shopping for?" He scowls. "Why the fuck would I waste money on a costume to just sit at home? I know you think we have all this money to just fucking waste on stupid shit but I actually have a real job, that I work hard at, to earn our money."

"You're right." I try to make myself as small as possible as his looming presence stalks towards me. I hate fighting with him. "I'm sorry."

"Fuck babe, sometimes you don't think at all, do you?" His large hand wraps tightly against my face, roughly tilting my head up so my eyes meet his. His fingers dig into my cheeks and tears well in my eyes at the pain. "Now go find a 'ho costume to match mine and we can get out of here. I'm meeting up with Will in like an hour." He releases me, the flesh he grabbed onto pulsing in pain. I'll definitely have bruises I'll need to cover tomorrow.

"You're going out tonight?" My voice comes out smaller—weaker—than I mean it to. "I was going to make dinner."

"You know I need guy time! I hate it when you're all clingy and shit. Go find a fucking costume and let's go." He dismisses me with a wave of his hand and I quickly shuffle away from him, desperate to get out of his orbit while he's in one of his moods.

I scan up and down the rows in the women's section for anything that looks like a whore costume. The idea tastes bitter on my tongue. I don't want to dress as a hooker. I want to dress in something that makes me feel bold, strong, fierce. But, I guess that's out of the question. I get to be Kyle's whore for the night, following him around from bar to bar as he flirts with other women. I can see now how our night will end—him shoving me face-first down into the mattress and closing his eyes while he fucks me from behind and imagines someone else. *Fucking wonderful.*

I round another row of costumes and see a woman scanning the shelves. She's beautiful. She is slightly taller than me, which probably puts her at around five-six or so, with long blonde hair styled in beautiful waves. Her body is curvy in all the right places. Her perfectly manicured, long red nails slide down the same red cloak I admired earlier. I can't seem to pull my eyes from her hand as it seductively strokes across the scarlet fabric. My tongue darts out to lick my bottom lip as I fixate on the path of her fingers, wondering what they'd feel like skimming across the sensitive flesh of my thighs. My pussy throbs at the thought.

What the heck is that? I'm not into girls. At least, I've never been before.

Sure, I can appreciate an attractive girl. Like, I can notice when another woman is more attractive than me but I've never wanted to *be* with another girl. But there's something about this woman that's pulling me in. Like there's a shimmering, invisible thread hooked into my core, pulling and twisting me towards the goddess in front of me. My eyes move upwards, slowly savoring her wide hips and plump breasts, the pale skin of her neck, and her beautifully full lips, before meeting her eyes. They're pale blue like the ocean, and full of alluring mischief. She caught me staring and yet, I don't care.

Pulling the costume from the rack, she approaches me silently. Her hips sway seductively as she walks and I can't help the pulse that thrums between my legs. I feel my panties dampen as she gets closer to me. *Holy Hell.* I've never felt like this before around another person.

When she's right in front of me, she stops. With her this close to me I can smell her. She smells like jasmine and vanilla. The sudden urge to lick up her throat and taste her strikes me.

What the hell? I can't go around licking strange women in Halloween stores!

"This would look beautiful on you." she says as she takes the cloak from the hanger and flings it behind me to rest on my shoulders. As she settles the cloak on me, her fingers lightly brush against my breast. Without knowing what I'm doing, my back bows out, arching for more of her touch against my sensitive skin. Suddenly, I'm desperate for her hands to be on me.

"No," I manage to choke out. "I'm not sexy enough for a costume like this." The words leave my mouth before I can stop them.

Her eyes flash with a moment of malice before her hands land on my hips, pulling me tightly against her. Her body is soft and warm and comforting. Every place her fingers touch me seem to hum with desire, as if she possesses the power to set each of my nerves on fire. She leans into me, gently brushing her lips against the shell of my ear. When she whispers to me, her warm breath sends shivers down my spine.

"I think you'd look radiant. In fact, I'd love to see you wearing this cloak and nothing else while I feast on your sweet little cunt."

Her words are filthy. I've never had anyone, female or male, talk to me that way. And I've certainly never had anyone *feast* on my private areas before. I should be horrified by what's happening but I can't deny the way my body responds to her with extraordinary need. My panties aren't damp, *they're drenched.*

"Tell me your name, princess. I need to know what name to call out later when I'm coming all over that beautiful face." Her voice is smooth like honey and I desperately want to hear her say more dirty things to me.

"Babe!" Kyle's voice carries across the store, breaking me from my trance before I can answer her. I pull away from the woman in front of me, disentangling myself from her. "I found it! This 'ho costume will be perfect!"

I swivel my head towards where he's calling from. "Alright! I'll be right there!"

When I turn back around, my mystery girl is gone.

CHAPTER THREE

Morgan

I can't stop thinking about that sweet little seductress. Her body felt so small and fragile against mine. I was tempted to throw her down, pull her dress up, and claim her right there in that fucking store. But then a male called to her. Of course, a beauty like that would be taken. It was foolish of me to even approach her. I'm supposed to be hunting for Victim Thirteen, which is why I'm at this stupid fucking place.

The lights are blinding me and the loud fucking music is giving me a headache. Clubs are one of the worst fucking inventions these idiot humans have created in recent years. I used to be able to find my victims at sweet little taverns. It was always quaint and warm, with good beer and food. The men would be traveling long distances with no one to miss them or come looking for them. It was so much easier back then. Now, I have to be thoughtful about my victims, look for men who won't have a lot of people asking too many questions when they disappear. I would like to take my time to find the perfect victim, but unfortunately, time isn't on my side. I need to feast on my final meal by Halloween, which is at the end of next week. My gift and my curse— eternal life and beauty but the price is thirteen corrupt souls before the rising of the blood moon. This year the blood moon falls right on Halloween. *Poetic as fuck right?*

So here I am, sitting on this uncomfortable stool, at this shitty downtown club, while waiting for the right man to approach. I down my drink, trying to drown all the fantasies about my sweet little princess that won't stop swirling around my mind. I need to focus. I can't have thoughts of tasting her cunt distracting me.

"Hey sexy, I haven't seen you around here before," a male whispers in my ear. His breath smells like stale beer and I can sense his intoxication immediately. He has piqued my interest.

Spinning on my stool to look at the fly I've caught in my web, I'm met with an average-looking male. He's not tall, but not short. Not fat, but certainly not in good shape, definitely not muscular enough to fight me off in my demon form. He would be considered stereotypically attractive to most. His hair is blonde and styled with enough gel to make it look disgustingly crunchy. He has a round baby face and slight stubble on his upper lip, telling me he's not too young but not too old. Maybe a college boy or fresh out of college. His hot pink polo, tropical shorts, and white flip-flops are ridiculous. We're in fucking Washington, not the tropics. He's obviously an ass.

He's perfect.

"Yeah," I flutter my eyelids seductively and recross my legs, drawing his attention down towards my short skirt. "I'm just in town for the week and wanted to have a little fun."

"Fun?" He leans toward me, pushing a loose lock of hair behind my ear. I pretend to blush but really I turn away because the overpowering smell of his body spray is gag-worthy. "I can certainly show you a little fun. Let me buy you a drink, pretty lady?"

Does that line actually work on anyone?

I have a rule about drinks— don't overindulge in them with victims. I've been burned before by males who drink too much and can't get it up. A flaccid dick does me no good. Intoxicated males are pliable and easy victims. Drunk males are angry and aggressive. This one has clearly had enough already.

"How about a dance instead?" I push my chest out, letting him get a glance at my very full bust. His eyes flick down to my breasts as he slowly licks his lips. He wants me. *Perfect.*

I allow him to take my hand and lead me to the dance

floor. The stench of stale alcohol and human body odor is overpowering out here in the middle of the crowded dance floor. The monster within snaps its jaws as it scents all the males surrounding me. It needs to be fed, and soon, before it gets out of hand.

He spins me, putting his front to my back. Swaying out of time with the music, he grinds against me as his hands explore my curves.

"You're really fucking hot," the man whisper-yells in my ear as his hands snake around my hips, pulling me flush against him.

No shit Sherlock.

He grinds his semi-hard cock against my ass. The monster in me stirs; its teeth pricking against the surface of my skin, anticipating sinking into the male behind me.

"You're not so bad yourself," I reply, tilting my head back and leaning against his chest as my eyes slip shut. If he thinks I'm more intoxicated than I am then he'll be willing to try something, and I desperately need him to try something.

Stuck drifting in a sea of sweaty human meat sacks, I let this man continue running his hands along my form. We sway off tempo to the pounding beat of the horrific music pumping into the club. His dick continues to thicken as his hands roam possessively across my curves. But it's not his touch I'm craving—not really. I can't get my mind off that sweet little thing I saw at the costume shop earlier. She looked so doe-eyed and innocent. Her dark hair and pale skin made her look like a fucking fairytale come to life. My sweet little princess, begging to be corrupted.

The thing that I can't fucking figure out though, is why she called to me like she did. The scent of her arousal hung so thickly in the air, it nearly choked me. My body screamed at me to take her right then and there. Lay her down, lick her sweet, slick pussy until she shattered and screamed for me. I wanted to ruin her for anyone else. But I can't suck from women. I'm a succubus for fuck's sake. I take from men. Never, not once in the thousands of years that I've been alive, has a woman called to me in that way. Sure, I've fucked women before, many women, but that's been just for fun. I've never wanted to claim a woman, possess a woman, completely fucking ruin a woman before. Not until *her*.

Suddenly I feel the male's hands creep under the hem of my skirt, pulling me from my wandering thoughts. I should stop him. I need to get him alone to do what I need. But with thoughts of my sweet little princess flitting across my vision, I close my eyes and let his fingers wander under my panties. I imagine it's her touching me, though. She'd be so shy at first, teasing me with small little touches until my pussy was a weeping mess for her.

He shoves a thick digit against my clit, rubbing me in an unsatisfying and overly aggressive way. My eyes pop open at the sudden intrusion. This male is clearly not skilled at pleasing women. I put my hand on his wrist to pull his hand off slightly, trying to coax him to rub me in a circular motion. He kind of gets the idea and I let myself sink back into my fantasy.

My sweet little princess is naked between my thighs, touching me where I need her most. Biting her lower lip in her teeth she looks at me from beneath those thick, dark lashes.

"Is that good?" she asks me, uncertainty laced in her tone while her soft little fingers stroke back and forth against my needy nub.

"Yes baby girl, just like that. You're doing so good for me."

My hips buck off the bed as she finds her rhythm and strokes me faster. Her petite tits heaving up and down as her breath quickens. The way she humps the empty air, desperate for some friction, tells me she's enjoying this as much as I am. Her delicate little fingers slide into me, stroking my inner walls.

"Do you want to taste me, princess?" I ask her, desperate for her to say yes.

"You want some fresh air?" The man behind me speaks and snaps me back into the moment. If I didn't need his cock so badly, I'd be furious at him for distracting me from the thoughts of my princess.

I was thoroughly enjoying my fantasy, thank you very much fuck-wad.

"Yeah," I manage to sound desperate for him when really, I'm desperate for someone completely different. But I don't need her. She's not what I'm supposed to be here for. "Yeah, let's get some fresh air out back."

Leading him through the writhing forms on the dance floor towards his doom, I can't help the anticipation bubbling through me. The strobes of purple and teal flash across the darkened room and the music shakes the floor below us as we weave through grinding couples. The mask of my beauty hides the true monster beneath. I turn and offer him a seductive smile. He thinks he's the hunter, but this poor little thing has no idea he's actually the prey.

Locating the fire exit in the back of the building, I push it open and am immediately hit by a blast of cold night air. Thankfully it's not raining, a miracle for Washington in the Fall, but it's still chilly out and the skimpy outfit I'm wearing is doing me no favors right now. A gentleman would offer me a coat, instead, this asshat aggressively pins me up against the brick exterior and forces his tongue down my throat.

Managing to push him off, I make an excuse to try to catch my breath and formulate a plan. "Wait! I don't even know your name."

He slams me back against the wall roughly, causing my head to hit the bricks. Stars dance on the corners of my vision and I blink rapidly, trying to clear them away. His hands grip me tightly as his mouth sucks on the tender skin of my neck. I manage to pry the suckerfish the fuck off my neck for a minute and shove him back again. I was going to be nice, but now I'm going to make this as painful as possible for him.

"You want my name, baby?" he asks as he fists my hair, causing a sharp gasp to leave my mouth. "When you come, you can scream out for Kyle."

Yeah, dude, you'll be the one screaming.

He shoves me to my knees. The loose pebbles and broken glass of the alleyway dig painfully into my knees and I squirm against the sharp sting, but he holds me tighter by my hair. His other hand moves to his belt. He stares down at me, a mixture of lust and hatred swirling in the gray of his irises.

"You're going to take my cock down your throat like a good little girl." Having undone his belt, he slowly slides his zipper down and frees his hardened length. It's average, just like the rest of him. I was hoping to go out this year with a bang—a real big, meaty cock that I could ride until I saw fucking stars—but beggars can't be choosers. And at this point, with how close we are to the blood moon, I'll take what I can get. "And then, maybe, I'll fuck your tight little slut hole."

Did this fucker just call my beautiful pussy a slut hole? Oh, he's so going to die a painful fucking death.

I open my mouth and stick out my tongue, allowing him to place his dick where he wants. As soon as there's physical contact, he throws his head back and moans.

Calm down, I haven't even done anything yet.

Sliding my tongue along the base, I pay special attention to where the crown meets the shaft. Precum beads on his tip and I suck it up with a satisfied moan. The monster within howls with delight at the first taste of our victim.

Hollowing out my cheeks, I take him fully into my mouth. The tip barely hits the back of my throat, it's not enough to really get me going. I need more. I need pain and pleasure wrapped together in a beautiful dichotomy to find my release. But he moans as if this is the best blowjob he's ever gotten.

"Yeah baby, just like that. You're doing so good for me sweet girl."

I'll show you sweet.

He's pounding against my face with hurried strokes. *Shit.* I need him to slow down. He's no good to me spilling down my throat.

Just as I'm about to ask him to fuck me the door swings open, the metal loudly hitting the brick wall behind us. A tall man looms in the open doorway, shrouded in shadows. His presence seems to suck the air from his surroundings, like a black hole straight to Hell. The monster inside me hisses. I can feel this new man's eyes burning into me as he watches me get throat fucked, my knees scrapped and bloodied in some shitty alley.

"*Dangerous man,*" my demon whispers inside my mind. "*Stay away.*"

I don't need to be told twice, this man is clearly a devil in sheep's clothing, not unlike myself, I suppose.

Takes a demon to know one.

"Come on man, we have to go," the new man states, not taking his eyes off me.

Blatantly ignoring his friend's request, Kyle thrusts deeper down my throat, causing warm tears to fall and slide down my cheeks.

"Not now man. This chick knows how to suck a cock like a fucking pro." The asshole with his cock buried in my throat turns desperate with his thrusts. No, this isn't what I need. I don't need him to blow his load down my fucking throat. I need to regain control here.

"Shit man, you know I like to watch but we've gotta go. There's a situation at the casino that I have to deal with." The man slides from the shadows and I catch a glimpse of his face in the shimmering moonlight. His features are fuzzy through my tears but from what I can tell, he's attractive. He has slick dirty blonde hair and piercing dark eyes. His jaw is chiseled and dusted with well-manicured stubble. He looks older than the man currently jackhammering my uvula but not by much. There's something unsettling about him though; his dark energy oozes danger.

Our new audience member reaches up to run a strand of my hair between his fingers, the beast within me roars in anger at his touch. I try to recoil but I'm held in place by Kyle's hands.

"Unless this pretty girl wants to come play with us,"

the new man questions as he leans so close to my face that I'm sure some of the spit welling up in the corners of my mouth must splatter on him.

No fucking way.

Kyle continues to relentlessly pound his cock down my throat while the newcomer slips his hand to my stiffened nipple. He flicks it with his finger as a sinister smirk spreads across his face.

"Tell me girlie, have you ever been filmed before? My audience would love to see those big ass titties bouncing up and down while you ride a cock. The pay is probably more than someone like you makes in a month."

Excuse you?

The thought of this evil man taking advantage of girls like that snaps something inside me. My anger boils, the monster within roaring to life. I slam both my fists into the man in front of me. His cock rips from my mouth as he tumbles backward. Before they can react, I jump to my feet and start backing away.

Kyle shoves his cock in his pants as they both laugh at me, his friend holding up his hands in surrender. "Alright, alright, got it. Very clearly not into it. But if you change your mind, you can find me at the Riverside Casino. Just ask for Will. I'd love to pay you for being such a good slut."

Oh no, he fucking did not.

"Fuck you!" I shout at them both. What assholes.

The man named Will spins back towards me. His eyes turn a shade of dark that I've known all too well from dangerous men—the type of men who like to hurt women. With each step he takes toward me, I take one back. I want to keep as much space between me and this devil as I can. When my back hits the alley wall behind me, fear and panic begin flooding my chest. Fuck, this is not good. He leans in and places both his hands against the wall behind me, caging me in. His canines glint in the moonlight as he sneers down at me.

"Or maybe, next time I catch you drinking alone at a bar, I'll make sure to put a little something extra in your cocktail. One of my special pills and you'll be more than willing to work for me, won't you? You'll spread those thick thighs and welcome a gang bang like a good little whore for me."

Before I can knee this fucker in the balls, he pushes off from the wall and spins back to his friend. They turn and walk back into the door to the club, laughing and clapping each other on the back. Little do they know, they just messed with the wrong fucking monster.

CHAPTER FOUR

Morgan

Note to self: skimpy little outfits are great for inside but when in Washington bring a raincoat along in case you need to stalk your victim afterwards. It's fucking wet and cold in this tree. My hair is soaked and clinging to my face. I can feel gloopy chunks of mascara running down my cheeks. I'm sure I look like a wet raccoon. *Fucking rain.* After this one, I'm headed somewhere sunny.

I followed motherfucker one and motherfucker two from the bar to this shithole apartment complex. My plan was to follow them to the casino, let them think I'd changed my mind, and then rip their fucking souls out of their bodies through their cocks as painfully as possible. My teeth are aching to sink into their cocks and feel their blood coating my insides. The rule is thirteen before the blood moon, but there's nothing against taking one extra. Asshole two would have just been a nice little bonus for the year and for my pussy. Unfortunately, when their truck stopped at this run-down building, Kyle hopped out and Will drove off, leaving me to decide which asshole I wanted to kill first. Lucky Kyle will be my victim thirteen, it seems.

Sometimes being an immortal and beautiful succubus is not a glamorous job. Case in point—my current situation. I'm thoroughly unimpressed with my new friend Kyle's living arrangements. It's a small grouping of apartments, with faded white siding and moss sprouting across the roof line. It looks as though they were built in the early nineties and haven't been updated since. The siding is faded in patches, with shingles that have been ripped away from the roof only to be replaced with fuzzy green moss. The windows look old and not insulated enough. I imagine it gets fucking cold in there during nights like tonight. It doesn't really get freezing here, but it's a wet, dreary type of cold that chills you down to the bone. Well, chills mortals down to their marrow. When you're an immortal succubus, the temperature is pretty irrelevant.

I'm sitting in one of the large fir trees that line the back of the building, allowing me a perfect view into his tiny apartment. He lives on the second of three stories, surrounded by neighbors on all sides. That normally would be a problem for me, with what I intend to do to him tonight, but this looks like the type of place where people don't ask questions about your comings and goings. It'll definitely work for what I have planned. The layout of the place seems to consist of a small, shitty kitchen attached to a barren living room with a small bedroom and bathroom off to the side. A sad little bachelor pad for a sad little man.

I wondered to myself how long it will take before someone notices the smell of Kyle's decomposing corpse in this shit-can apartment complex and calls the cops to investigate. It doesn't matter, really. By the time they come, I'll be long gone.

A twinge of something pulls at my core at the thought of leaving this city. Regret? Guilt? Pain? *What the hell?* I'm a succubus for fuck's sake. I travel from town to town sucking men's souls through their dicks. I don't stay in one place, not for longer than needed anyway.

"*Then take her with us,*" the demon's voice curls through my mind like wisps of smoke.

No. She was nothing more than a chance, insignificant encounter.

I refocus my attention back on Kyle. After being dropped off by his friend, he went upstairs, grabbed a cheap beer from his refrigerator, and plopped his ass down on his worn-out couch. I climbed to a branch not two feet from his window and watched as he turned on porn and started stroking himself. I should barge in and take what I need from him, but I can't seem to pull my eyes from the screen he is watching. The video he's jacking off to shows some busty blonde girls, so similar in looks that they could be clones, playing with each other.

The image of the two women touching and pleasing one another has my mind wandering back to *her*. I imagine myself lying on the bed with her on top of me, rubbing her needy cunt against mine as our tongues fight against one another for dominance. I wonder if she's ever eaten pussy before.

Would she eat mine if I asked her real nicely?

I lose myself thinking about how good those pouty little red lips would feel wrapped around my slit, licking and sucking my clit until I came all over her beautiful face. The image of her perfect little form between my legs makes my pussy drip and throb with a need like I've never felt before. I have to stop myself from falling out of the tree as my hips roll in a desperate urge to relieve some of this tension the mere thought of her has building inside me. *Fuck. What is this girl doing to me?*

I can't handle any more thoughts of her and her soft, luscious lips that I'm desperate to taste. I need to focus. I need to claim my thirteenth victim or there is no future for me, with or without her.

Suddenly the door to his apartment slams open, pulling me from my thoughts. Kyle continues to jack himself, not even bothering to turn and see who has entered the apartment. But it isn't him I'm watching. No, my eyes are glued on the form in the doorway. Her petite frame and jet-black hair make her barely a wisp of life amongst the shadows. Her eyes flare with anger as she looks at the man on the couch. Fuck, her fire is intoxicating. I'm struck with the urge to stoke that fire and let it consume me completely. I'm like a damn moth drawn to her flame, unable to rip myself away from her pull. But just as quickly as the fire burst within her, it extinguishes. She bows her head and moves to hang up her coat and purse.

Why the hell is my princess here? With him? Looking submissive to this shit stain of a human?

The demon roars to life inside me, demanding I storm inside and steal his soul while she watches before claiming her as mine.

Mine.

Shaking my head, I will the monster to calm down. She's not mine. *Not yet, anyway.* I need to know why she's here, in his apartment.

Is this the male she's with? The one who called her away from me earlier?

No, It can't be. The thought sends anger shooting through my veins. The thought that he'd cheat on such a perfect creature—letting random women suck his dick in a dirty alley while she waits at home for him—makes me see red. If he wasn't dead meat before, he certainly is now.

And then she'll be all mine to take and have and own.

Would it scare her away if I feasted on him in front of her though? *Probably*. I don't want to scare her so badly that she runs from me. I want to be able to savor her fear.

My sweet princess moves into the kitchen and grabs a glass of water. Just as she tilts her head back to take a gulp, movement in the corner of my eye catches my attention. Kyle is on the move, stalking across the room towards my girl. A sweet little tabby cat rubs its body against my girl's legs, glaring at the man stalking silently toward them as if trying to warn its owner of the evil approaching.

Good kitty.

My girl doesn't seem to notice the clear warning, and I watch as Kyle grabs her roughly by the back of her neck. She chokes on her water and spits all over the kitchen counter in front of her. The cat is still between her legs. Its paw swipes out to claw at the man assaulting its owner. I watch in horror as Kyle shoves my girl down, hitting her face against the countertop, and then kicks the cat out of the way. Before I can think I'm on my feet, bracing against the tree trunk for balance as I gauge how hard I'll need to jump to break through their window.

Fuck. No, I can't. If I charge in there like some fucking succubus superhero I'll scare her away. *Shit*.

Kyle is leaning over her now, spitting words against her face that I can't hear. Gone is the smooth-talking pretty boy from the club. Now, his face is contorted into an ugly shade of masculine fury. He's drunk. Drunk and mean and horny. It's not a good combination.

Tears fall from my sweet girl's beautiful eyes and roll down her pale cheeks. Fuck me, the urge to storm in there and lick the tears from her face is overwhelming. She'd cry so pretty for me with my fingers deep inside her tight little cunt. I bet she tastes delicious. She deserves to be worshiped and pleasured, not beaten and abused. Anger like I haven't known in centuries crawls beneath my skin and boils in my veins.

I decide right then and there to steal her from him and make her mine. I will rip his soul from his body as painfully as possible, then fuck her in his blood. The last thing he'll see in his pathetic little life is me making her shatter in pleasure. Something I'm sure he's never done.

First, I need to get rid of this motherfucker and suck his sick, shitty soul out of him. I can see how much pressure he's putting on her from here, her face is completely smashed against the countertop as he struggles with his pants. He's trying to pull them all the way down with one hand, drunkenly fumbling over his own ass.

I can't watch this. I'll fucking rip him limb from limb right now if he hurts her.

Maybe if I had finished him off earlier, he wouldn't be here taking it out on her. Guilt racks through my entire body and I feel as though I'm going to be sick if I have to watch him take what's not willingly given to him just because he can. She might be smaller than him but that doesn't mean he has any right to take from her.

She tries to shove him off by bucking her hips against the counter and pushing at his hand. I still can't hear anything, but it looks like she's pleading with him to stop or at least be gentler. Like all other asshole males, he doesn't respond well to pleading. Spinning her to face him upright, he brings his hand down across her face. She recoils back, holding her hands up to block the next blow. He hits her again and something in me snaps. I may not want to scare her away but there's no way in hell I can sit here and watch my girl be beaten and raped.

I might need a thirteenth victim, but I need her just as badly, if not more. I'm willing to wait to claim Kyle's soul if it means keeping her safe. I'm about to fuck up his night.

Ripping off a branch from above me, I hold onto the tree with one hand and throw the branch with my other as hard as I can. The jagged wood shatters through the window, scattering shimmering pieces of glass across the apartment floor. There's some beauty in the violent scene in front of me as the world seems to slow and shift with each cascading shard. The crash breaks through the silence of the night and stops Kyle in his tracks. As quickly as I can, I shift over to the next branch, hiding myself behind the trunk of the tree and praying no one saw me. I can't afford any trouble, not this close to the blood moon.

With the window blown out, I can hear Kyle's footsteps crunching over the glass and her heavyhearted sobbing in the background. The sound nearly rips my heart from my chest. The only tears she should be spilling are tears of pleasure I pull from her.

"What the fuck was that?" Kyle screams, clearly furious about the giant tree branch that just went flying through his window. "The landlord is going to be hearing from me first thing tomorrow! These windows are so shitty that a tree branch can just knock them out? Is he fucking kidding me? He doesn't know who he's dealing with! I will *own* him, fucking own him!"

Kyle continues his rant at no one, screaming into the night, but I don't hear him. My focus is on the shadow running across the parking lot ahead of me. She runs silently on swift feet to a beat-up old sedan. She moves efficiently and effortlessly, like she's done this before and knows the routine. Without turning on her lights, she backs out of the spot and drives away, leaving chaos and pain behind her.

"Babe, call the landlord now! He needs to get his ass out here tonight to fix this!" Kyle yells at the empty apartment behind him, oblivious to the fact that she's run off into the safety of the shadows. "Babe?"

He spins, finally noticing the apartment is empty and he's talking to no one.

"What in the actual *fuck*? Did that bitch take off? You've

got to be fucking kidding me?"

I'm really glad I fucked up this prick's night.

A sudden thump next to me has the hairs on the back of my neck standing up. Something is in the tree with me, I can feel it. It can't be Kyle, he's too big and definitely not limber enough to make that jump. It's decidedly *not* something human. My Hellish hackles raise in defense, my human skin falling away slightly to reveal the monster within.

With my heart beating erratically and the air struck in my lungs, I move slowly to peek around the trunk of the tree. What meets my eyes on the other side of the tree trunk surprises me. It takes me a moment to register that the two slanted, glowing eyes appraising me belong to a cat. *Her fucking cat.* The orange tabby sits on a branch staring right at me as if it can see straight through to my soul. *Fucking cats.*

"You're coming with me aren't you?"

The cat doesn't answer—I mean it can't, it's a cat—but it tilts its head slightly to the side. The slits of its eyes narrow at me. I've lived long enough to know not to mess with cats. They're animals full of instinct, magic, and fury. There's a reason why witches always choose them as familiars, I suppose.

Usually, cats hate me. They seem to be largely opposed to the Hell demon residing in my soul. This one, however, seems to believe it's coming with me. I have a feeling it has something to do with my princess.

"Alright, come on. Let's get the fuck out of here."

The furry beast walks gracefully across the branch and willingly allows me to pick him up. He's surprisingly light. His warmth is comforting tucked in under my arms.

I may not have what I came for, but at least my girl's safe for the night. That stunning and broken creature is *mine*. She may not know it yet but I feel it in my soul, this consuming need to claim her—possess her. And I'm sure as shit not letting some asshole with a very average dick get in the way of me claiming what's mine.

Now, I just need to find her.

CHAPTER FIVE

Scarlett

"I'll take a large pumpkin spice latte, extra pumpkin spice, extra whip cream, and nonfat," the woman in front of me demands before placing her phone back up to her ear to continue her annoyingly loud conversation.

I could warn her that there's no way any part of that drink will be low in fat, but she's too busy complaining to the person on the other end of the line about how bitchy one of her coworkers is. My guess? She's the bitch. She's a typical type of difficult customer: covered in head-to-toe designer athletic gear, fake blonde hair, platform shoes that are definitely not athletic, and a fanny pack strapped across the front of her chest. There's no point in arguing with customers like this. You just give them what they asked for, pray they don't complain, and send them out into the world to terrorize other poor customer service workers. I smile softly with my head turned down and walk away.

The machine in front of me whirs and buzzes as I approach. There was once a time when I was intimidated by the giant, stainless steel espresso machine, but now it feels comforting and familiar to stand behind the safety of its steam. I grab the jug of nonfat milk and slosh it into the steel mug before turning on the steam wand. The steamed milk whispers as the liquid spins and swirls. Satisfied with my foam, I drop the milk mug and let it continue warming. I move to the espresso grinder, clicking it three times to deposit the bitter powder from the hopper into the portafilter. Sliding the espresso filled cup into the machine, I place the shot glasses underneath and push the button. The machine churns and sputters as hot water pushes through the grinds, creating a tiny waterfall of caffeinated goodness. I pump eight pumps of the goopy pumpkin spice syrup into the cup and internally cringe. This is going to be a sugar bomb. Turning off the steam wand, I check that my shots are beautifully layered before dumping them over the syrup and swirling. I only have a moment before the shots die so I quickly add the warm milk, making sure to leave enough room for extra, extra whip cream.

"Large, nonfat, extra whip, pumpkin spice latte," I call out as I place the paper cup on the counter. The customer is too busy prattling into her phone to even acknowledge my smile or thank me. She grabs her drink and settles at one of the small round tables littered around the little cafe.

I know it's silly, but I take pride in each and every drink. Being a barista isn't a fancy career, it isn't glamorous, but I love it. I love the precision and the detail. I love making latte art and experimenting with drinks. There's talent to a good cup of coffee and I secretly like to think of myself as a little latte artist. It's stupid, but for me, it's comforting. And after last night, I could use some comfort.

Kyle's been rough with me before, sure, but he's never scared me like that. I was so convinced he was going to force himself further on me in our kitchen. There've been plenty of times when I gave in and allowed him inside me, even when I wasn't in the mood. But last night felt different. It felt worse—scarier. It can't be rape if it's your boyfriend though, right? I know he'll be pissed that I ran away but I needed to get out of there.

I stayed with my friend Sam. She works at the coffee shop with me and has been my friend for years. She stopped asking questions after I showed up at her door for the tenth time, always late at night, always with bruises and tears staining my cheeks. At first, she tried to convince me to leave him, but that would be like leaving my life. Where would I live? What would I do about rent money? I'd need an apartment that would accept pets so I could bring Samson. No, it'd be too messy. Eventually, she gave up trying to convince me to leave. Now, she just opens the door silently for me when I come knocking late at night. I never miss the look of pity in her eyes though. This time I didn't even have a chance to grab Samson before I left. Usually, the feline is always right at my feet, my little orange shadow, but he must have been scared by the loud crash of the window breaking and ran to hide. I'm worried about him; a sense of gnawing anxiety has been bothering me all day long. I plan to go check on him and make up with Kyle after my shift.

"Excuse me!" I'm ripped from my thoughts as a shrill voice rings across the small space of the cafe.

Coming back from around the espresso machine to the front counter, I'm met with a death glare. Miss large pumpkin spice latte, nonfat, with extra whipped cream is glaring at me from the other side of the counter. She looks pissed. *Fuck!* She must have ended her phone call, leaving her undistracted and able to focus all her angry energy straight towards me. *Joy.*

"Hello, ma'am. How may I assist you?" I put on my nicest voice, trying to placate her.

I quickly glance around the shop, looking for anyone who might be able to save me. Sadly, it's just the two of us and a few elderly male patrons sipping their black coffee and reading their newspapers in the back of the shop. My manager, Kim, ran to the bank just a minute ago. She'll be gone for at least another thirty minutes. I'm on my own to deal with her. *Fan-fucking-tastic.*

"Are you fucking kidding me with this shit? I asked for a pumpkin spice latte. I don't know what the fuck you made, but this is unsatisfactory. And there's barely any whip cream!" she spits at me, her voice laced with venom.

I want so desperately to tell her to take her shitty attitude and fuck right off. But, that would not really be the best for my employment status. So, I put on the kindest smile I can muster in the face of this small angry woman.

"I'm so sorry you don't like your drink, ma'am. I'd be happy to remake it for you if you'd like?"

Her brown eyes scan my face, looking for what, I don't know. They're the color of shit. She's an ugly woman with an angry scowl contorting her face and cold condescension radiating off her in waves.

"I order this same drink at Starbucks every single morning and it's always the same. But the *one* day I decide to be a good person and patronize a small business, you have to fuck it up. I expect you to remake it and offer me a gift certificate for my trouble!"

"I'm so sorry you were unhappy with your drink, ma'am. But, we use a different syrup than Starbucks so it might taste slightly different. I'd be happy to remake it but it's never going to taste exactly like theirs."

She sucks in a long, loud breath. Her eyes widen with

fury, and I know I'm in for it now.

"Listen to me you stupid fucking cunt," she spits, leaning across the counter. "I'm sure you're too idiotic to understand this but I know what my drink is supposed to taste like and it's your job to make that drink. If you fuck this up again, I'll destroy your little shithouse coffee shop all over social media. I have over a thousand followers and I'm sure they'd love to hear my review of your shop."

It's not my coffee shop you dumb bitch.

"I understand ma'am. I can see you're upset. I'm happy to remake your drink for you but no matter what I do, it will never taste just like Starbucks." I'm walking a dangerous line here and I know it. If I argue with her she might lose it, but if I make her another non-Starbucks drink, she also might lose it. *Yay for customer service jobs, right?*

Hot and crazed anger blooms across her face. She looks like she might jump across the counter and throttle me. I take a step back. But instead of jumping the laminate barrier, she takes the lid slowly off her drink, exposing the sugary, hot liquid within.

"How dare you talk back to me you fucking piece of shit little—" her arm swings backward and down. I register that she's going to throw the drink at me and I start to move out of the way to try to avoid it.

Suddenly, a hand grabs her wrist and stills her motions. Sharp, blood-red nails dig into the woman's skin, making her veins pop up against the thin barrier of her fake-tanned flesh.

"You will put that drink down and apologize to her right now." A low and calm voice breaks the tense silence.

Standing there, holding the wrist of my angry customer in her fierce claws, is the woman from the costume shop. Her eyes are trained on the woman across the counter from me, a fiery blaze flicking through her gaze. She's wearing a tight, shimmering, white dress that pulls against her ample breasts and hips. Her dress shines in the streak of sunlight coming in through the window, slightly blinding me momentarily. I wonder for a fleeting moment if she might be an angel from the way she seems to glow. She's the same height as the other woman but her imposing presence makes her seem larger, like all the light is sucked from the room and funneled straight to her. Her scent—jasmine and vanilla—tickles my nose, overpowering even the strong aroma of coffee that usually clings to the air in here.

Fuck me. She's fucking gorgeous.

I thought she was beautiful the first time I saw her but the way she seems to radiate with power makes her look like a goddess. A fiery, powerful, sexy as fuck female. *Who needs a white knight when you can have a goddess in glitter coming to save you, right?*

"Excuse me?" My least favorite customer rounds on my savior. "Get your fucking hands off me, you bitch!"

"I will release you," she says, her voice deadly calm—

too calm. She's like a predator, slowly working her prey back into a corner. "But when I do, you will apologize, take your drink, and go."

My goddesses' eyes finally flick to mine and my entire body lights on fire. She's so beautiful it hurts. Her blonde hair is styled in soft waves that frame her heart-shaped face. Her blue eyes remind me of the waves of the sea, shifting and swirling on a clear day. Her lips are covered with a sheer pink gloss that makes them look absolutely irresistible. The sudden urge to crash my lips against hers and taste her crosses my mind.

Now's probably not a good time for that though.

"And who the fuck do you think you are?" bitchy-customer-lady yells.

A slow and sinister smirk spreads across my savior's face. Her eyes seem to shift in color slightly, they're still the color of a calm sea, but now they seem to be ringed with red. *Shit.*

Her nails dig into the customer's wrist, blood pooling where the sharp edges are digging into the other woman's skin.

"Ow! What the fuck?" she shrieks, her panicked eyes flicking back and forth between her now bloodied wrist and my eyes, as if I'm going to save her. *Yeah right, bitch.* "Stop please!" Blood drips from her wrist onto the hardwood floors beneath her. "Fine! Fine! I'll leave! Just please let go!"

"I will let go when you apologize to the kind and beautiful woman behind the counter."

"Fine! Fuck! Fine. I'm sorry, okay?" The woman rips her wrist away, spilling her latte all over herself in the process. She doesn't even seem to care. She just runs for the door.

The beautiful goddess in front of me watches her prey scurry away hastily. An amused smirk plays across her features. There's something about her that is so hypnotizing, it's as if I couldn't pull my gaze from her even if I wanted to. I don't want to though, she's the most beautiful woman I've ever seen.

The fleeing customer throws the door open, casting one last fearful glance over her shoulder. The radiant woman in front of me gives her a wave of her bloodied fingers before telling her in a sugary sweet voice, "And don't come back soon!"

I cover my mouth to avoid exposing the smile that's spread across my face.

The customer is so busy fleeing that she collides into my manager as she exits the door. She plows straight into Kim, before running swiftly into the rainy parking lot without so much as an apology or second glance.

Kim enters the coffee shop with a perplexed look on her face. My manager takes in the bloodied floor and spilled latte. "What the hell happened here?"

Before I can answer her and apologize for the mess, the other woman does. "That customer was being rude, aggressive, and offensive towards your employee. I intervened to ask her to leave. I apologize if it caused any inconvenience to your shop, I was simply trying to remind that woman that customer service employees don't deserve to be treated as second class citizens." She flashes my boss a sincere smile that radiates warmth and kindness.

It's such a stark contrast to the powerful and fierce woman who stood before me a moment ago. I wonder if there is something unsavory about my new friend.

Kim's eyes flick to me. She assesses me. I'm sure I look like a mess. That whole interaction was…a lot.

"Scarlett, are you alright?"

"Fine," I manage to squeak out. My voice is small and hesitant. I hate how weak I am sometimes.

"Why don't you go take a break? Have some water, okay?"

I nod my head in agreement, lifting my apron up and over my head. I begin to turn to walk down the length of the workspace behind the counter when a hand grabs my arm. I spin to find the beautiful woman, my goddess, staring at me intensely.

"Have a cup of coffee with me while you take a break?"

I should say no. There's something about this woman that seems slightly dangerous. I mean, she just made a customer bleed all over the floor because they were rude to me. The way she stares at me, with such intensity, makes me feel as though I might spontaneously combust right where I stand. And yet, I can't seem to pull myself out of her orbit.

She's like the fucking sun and I want to gravitate closer and closer to her, letting her pull me in. I desperately want her eyes and hands to stay on me and never leave.

"Okay," I manage to whisper. "I'll grab two cups of coffee."

"Keep mine black, princess." She winks at me before stalking off towards a secluded table up in the loft space.

Holding the warm porcelain mug carefully between my hands, I make my way up the steep steps. The loft area is set back at the very far end of the shop, opposite the register but tucked into the roofline in such a way that it creates a private little retreat. Not many customers choose to brave the steep, open-tread steps, leaving the area an awkward and rarely used space. It's my favorite part of the shop though. The entire back wall is composed of windows, giving the illusion that the light wood floors simply drop you off into the ocean beyond. On clear summer days, I've seen orcas splashing in the water from these windows. I usually take my breaks up here because it feels calm and quiet and safe.

As I reach the top of the steps I see that today is not unlike most. It's pretty much empty up here. However, one seat is taken.

My beautiful savior sits at a small, round, two-person table tucked right up against the floor-to-ceiling windows.

She's looking out at the ocean. Her blonde hair hangs like a shimmering curtain around her face and down her shoulders. Her shimmery dress against her tanned skin is stunning. I wish I could look like her—poised and put together. She's radiant.

I hesitate as I round the banister, uncertain if I should approach her. She did tell me to join her for a coffee, but she looks so peaceful. And she doesn't even know me. What if when we start talking she finds me super boring, or I say the wrong thing? Then we'd be stuck up here in awkward silence. Ugh.

As if she can sense my thoughts, she turns to face me. When she spots me, a bright smile lights up her face. She's even more gorgeous when she smiles. She shines like the god-damned sun; further pulling me into her orbit. She's stunning, so much so it makes my palms start to sweat. A lump forms in my throat. I'm not used to having someone's attention focused solely on me. It's a bit unnerving.

"Come sit with me?" She motions to the chair across from her, inviting me to join her.

Part of me wants to run and hide. I worry my bottom lip between my teeth, picking at the dried pieces of skin. I'm too used to mean girls who pretend to be nice then rip you apart and make you feel like shit. I've never been pretty and popular. I'm not one of those types of girls. I bet this girl in front of me has always been popular. The way she lights up a room and draws people in, I imagine she's always been the center of everyone's focus. I have no idea what she wants with someone like me. Why would she even be wasting her time sitting and waiting for me?

But, I can't deny her.

"Thanks," I mumble as I slip a loose strand of dark hair behind my ear and shuffle across the rustic wooden floor.

I grab the back of the black chair across from her. It slightly scrapes against the floor as I pull it out and plop down on it. I barely look up as I slide the warm mug of black liquid across the table towards her.

"You didn't get anything for yourself?" she asks as her hands wrap around mine, trapping my fingers between the warmth of the mug and the heat of her touch.

When her skin makes contact with my own flesh it's as though I've been shocked. Electricity skitters across my nerves making my insides come to life. I pull my hand back quickly to avoid the abnormal sensation her touch elicits. I don't want to *want* this woman's touch as desperately as I seem to. My mind is telling me that she may be dangerous and slightly unhinged. My body, on the other hand, seems to crave her with every single ounce of desire it can muster.

What the hell is happening to me?

When I look up, my eyes meet hers. I'm blown away by the beauty of her gaze. She's somehow soft and hard; mysterious, yet comfortable. She's such an anomaly and a part of me wonders what it would be like to truly belong to this woman.

She cocks her head to the side, a slight smirk pulling at the corner of her full pink lips. It's only then I realize that she asked me a question, and like a fucking idiot I've been sitting here gawking at her instead of answering.

"Sorry. What?"

"I said," she begins with a slight laugh in her tone that makes my stomach flip in a very abnormal way, "you didn't bring a coffee up here for yourself?"

"Oh, no. I already had enough today." It's true, I've already made myself multiple espresso based drinks today. If I keep drinking caffeine, I'll be a jittery mess. Espresso on tap is the blessing and the curse of being a barista.

"What about some food? Water?" Her eyes narrow faintly as she assesses me. She seems to be sizing me up. Inspecting me. For what, though? I have no idea.

"I'm good," I mumble as I pull at the loose threads on the edge of my dark-knitted cardigan.

My style has always been a little alternative. While other girls were wearing Abercrombie & Fitch pink tee shirts and tight jeans, I opted for alternative grandma chic. Oversized sweaters, black dresses and skirts paired with fishnets, and black combat boots are kind of my uniform, so to speak. Some people used to call me goth or emo as an insult but it never really offended me. I like my alternative style. I'm not trying to be anyone I'm not.

I've never felt as self-conscious as I do right now, sitting across from the most beautiful woman I've ever seen in real life. Here I am in coffee-stained Chucks and she's sitting across from me in an angelic shimmering dress and high heels. I can feel her eyes on me, traveling across my turned-down face and slumped shoulders. Heat stings my cheeks as the weight of her gaze roams across my skin. I wish I'd put on more make-up or done my hair—something.

The sound of wood dragging catches my attention and I look up to see her moving her chair around the table. She slides the chair right next to mine and sits gracefully. Our thighs brush and I can't stop the summersaults my stomach seems to do in response.

"I'm Morgan," her voice is like a soft purr across my soul, so smooth and seductive.

"Scarlett," I mumble, keeping my eyes fixated on my lap, unable to meet her searing stare.

She leans in close to me and her distinct scent fills my nose. She smells like an intoxicating mix of vanilla and jasmine. It's what I imagine a witch or a siren would smell like. It's magical and alluring, yet also dangerous. Everything about her seems slightly dangerous, but I can't help feeling like her kind of danger would be worth the risk.

"You have to take care of yourself, Scarlett." Her fingers skate up and down my thigh in a hypnotically soothing rhythm. Her touch in such an intimate area of my body sends sparks straight to my core.

I don't want her to ever stop touching me.

"Let me guess," she leans into me as she speaks and her nearness is both comforting and anxiety provoking. I wipe my sweaty palms on the insides of my sweater sleeves. "You're the type that takes care of everyone else?"

I lift my eyes and am met with her intense stare. Looking into her blue eyes is like looking into the depths of the ocean—both alluring and alarming. I simply nod. She's right, but saying it feels…vulnerable.

Her fingers skirt higher and higher up my thigh, dangerously close to where I desperately do, and do not, want them to go.

"And who takes care of you?" She cocks her head as she speaks, challenging me to stop her.

"No—No one," I manage to choke out. She seems to have stolen all the air from the room and I can't get my lungs to gasp a full breath.

"Everyone needs someone to care for them. When you're down you deserve to have someone who will hold your hand and pull you back onto your feet. You deserve to be taken care of, princess."

Her words strike a chord deep down somewhere in my soul. It cracks open something I didn't even know was chipped.

"Maybe you need something—someone—different.

Someone who can make you feel something…new." Her fingers are skimming dangerously high up my thigh. Her words, her touch, her mere presence is driving me insane. I want her so badly it hurts. The pulsing ache between my thighs is so intense I feel as though I might spontaneously combust at any moment.

"Yes," I manage to whisper on a jagged exhale.

"Tell me, lovely, have you ever kissed a girl before?" Her words send a jolt of electricity straight to my needy core.

I've never had the urge to kiss another girl before.

But I've also never been as absolutely desperate to kiss someone as I am right now.

"No."

As soon as the single word leaves my lips, she removes her hand from my thigh. My stomach drops from the loss of her touch. But just as quickly as her fingers leave my thigh, they find their way to my chin, gently turning my face so that I'm looking directly at her. Her eyes are filled with a blazing fire. I press my thighs together tightly, trying to alleviate the ache her heated gaze and suggestive words are eliciting.

"Do you want to?"

Her eyes track the path of my tongue as I lick across my bottom lip. The way she looks at me, like she'd consume me entirely, is so addictive that I'm not sure I'll make it out of this moment unscathed. And when I nod, giving her consent, she strikes.

Her hand cups my cheek as she roughly pulls me towards her. Her lips meet mine with a gentle ease I've never felt before. Kissing her is so soft and sweet. It's so different from kissing Kyle, or any other boy I've ever kissed. Her lips cushion mine in a gentle and consistent pattern that has me involuntarily moaning against her. There's hunger but it's as if she's begging, not taking. Her taste is amazing. It's a seductive mix of vanilla and powdered sugar. At first I'm shy, tentative about kissing another girl, but when her tongue lightly brushes along my lips, I instantly part my lips allowing her inside.

Her tongue skims so lightly over mine. It's like she's teasing me. Each short stroke of her tongue causes the ache between my thighs to grow even more. My nipples are hard and painfully needy as she expertly deepens our kiss. I never want this kiss to stop, and yet, I'm desperate to know how her tongue would feel against other parts of my body.

Then, just as suddenly as she started, she stops. I'm left breathless and wanting as she pulls away. I look up at her in confusion. A smirk pulls at the corner of her mouth. She reaches out to push a piece of dark hair behind my ear.

"So fucking beautiful," she mutters before slinging back the remainder of her coffee, pushing back from the table, and walking away.

I'm left desperate and confused as I watch my goddesses' seductive hips sway out of sight.

CHAPTER SIX

Morgan

I've waited centuries for this, but it feels like I've been waiting an eternity for her. I haven't felt this need—this desire—for someone in so long. Not since *him*, the man that broke my heart. I was starting to worry that selling my soul to the Devil meant that I'd given up any shot at love. But now there's *her*.

Maybe this isn't love…not yet. But this possessive obsession I feel can only end in one of two ways: we will get our happily ever after or be consumed by complete destruction. I'm hoping this time someone doesn't end up roasting for all eternity in the pits of Hell.

It was torture to pull myself from her earlier. She tasted like caramel—rich and sweet and so sinfully seductive. I knew that I wanted her but I did not anticipate the hunger which kissing her would elicit within me. I was so close to laying her down on that tiny little table and licking her deliciously tight cunt until she came all over my face. What I wouldn't have given to hear that breathy little moan I pulled from her turned into screams of ecstasy. But I had to pull back. I couldn't risk scaring her…at least not yet.

The thing is, I don't just want this girl—I *need* her. Her moans, her screams, her pleasure, her pain–I want them all. I *need* them all.

She's mine.

She just doesn't know it yet.

I can tell she wants me too. I could see the heated desire swirling through her blown out pupils after our kiss. I could smell how fucking wet her pretty pussy was for me. She was so fucking eager. She'll be my perfect little pet.

She just doesn't understand yet how absolutely *possessive* I can be about what's mine.

If she thinks I'll just let her run on home to Kyle, she's mistaken. I left her needy and wanting for a reason. No one, especially not her shit-stain, soon to be ex-boyfriend, is going to be taking care of that ache between her thighs. From now on, I'm the only one that will taste her; I'm the only one that will touch her.

Anyone who tries to lay a finger on what's mine won't just punch their ticket to Hell, but will be hand delivered there by me.

Which is why I'm following her, of course. Kyle will be dying either way, but it'll be sooner rather than later, if he lays a finger on her.

I really should be focused on finding my thirteenth victim. Time is running out. If he pushes it tonight, maybe I can kill two birds with one stone—get him as my victim and claim my precious princesses' cunt as mine.

I don't want her to see me that way though. I want her to see the seductive and attractive side of me. The side of me she's drawn to. I'll have to be creative in order to hide from her what I truly am. She can never know that underneath my beautiful exterior is a demon. After all, who'd want to share their life—their heart—with a demon?

To my great relief, I followed her not back to her little apartment where she resides with Kyle, but to a lovely little house on the opposite side of town. It's a cute, blue, two-story townhouse in a sweet suburban neighborhood. So charming. So safe.

Not a great place for stalking a girl though.

Luckily, a voluptuous young woman doesn't give off "creepy masked stalker" vibes. Despite the rain, I leave the hood of my dark sweatshirt down so everyone can see what a threat I *don't* appear to be. Humans are dumb. They assume all monsters look monstrous; they're too vain to realize that sometimes even Hell demons come in pretty packages. Which is why no one bats an eye as I creep through their neighborhood and waltz right into a stranger's backyard.

Quietly opening the back gate, I slip through it and into the quaint little garden behind the townhouse. It's lush and green with large trees, just like it always is in the Pacific Northwest. It's a perfect place to hide.I make myself comfortable behind a large floral bush that provides that perfect amount of cover while still being able to peer into the large and illuminated windows. Well, as comfortable as I can get squatting in a bush in the rain.

I take my bag from my shoulder and gently place it on the ground, careful of the package hidden inside.

Scarlett is sitting at a table with another woman. The other girl is short and curvy with mousy brown hair. She's not unattractive but clearly not as attractive as I am. Plus, Scarlett said she'd never kissed a woman before. I don't think she'd lie to me about that, right? It must just be her friend she's staying with. But, fucking hell, that doesn't stop me from becoming a jealous fucking mess as I watch *my* princess laugh at something the other girl just said. I want to be the reason she laughs just as badly as I want to be the reason she screams and cries.

I want it all with this girl.

Her chest rises and falls as she laughs, causing her tits to bounce. They're so fucking perfect—perky and just the right size for me to palm in my hand. My pussy dampens as my mind wanders to images of her naked and desperate beneath me. I wonder if her nipples will be tiny little pink buds or large and erect, begging to be sucked.

Fuck, I want her so desperately.

I watch as the girls clean up their dinner and move to a different room of the house. I can no longer see them from where I'm crouched.

Where the hell did they go? What the fuck are they doing?

This isn't going to work. I need her too badly. My obsession with her is too intense. I can't just watch.

"*Get her. Take her. Claim her,*" the demon within me whispers. I can sense how badly he wants to get his claws into her. If I let him, he'd surely devour her.

I slowly start to ascend from the bushes, ready to find my girl, but movement catches my eye. Sinking back into the shadowed cover of my hiding place, I watch as Scarlett's lithe form gracefully makes her way down the hall. She moves so smoothly, each stride is like the flow of waves dancing in the sea. She exudes a type of feminine energy that's absolutely mesmerizing. She's regal. A type of woman that is timelessly ethereal and captivating. Every soft sigh and each swing of her delicate hips has me wanting to know how sweet and submissive she'd be beneath me.

She disappears for another moment before a bedroom light flips on right in front of me. I sink deeper into the shadows, careful to not let her see me. I have a front row seat to her unknowing striptease as she lifts her shirt off and throws it into the hamper in the corner. Her cleavage is plump and firm, aching to be bitten.

Her arms reach behind her back to release her white lace bra. Her beautiful breasts burst free from their confinement. They're perfect. They're round and pale and perky. Her nipples are so pink and pretty. I feel my pussy clench at the sight, desperate to feel the stiffened buds against my tongue.

"*Mine*," the demon whispers again across my mind. He's as desperate to taste her as I am.

I watch, licking my lips in anticipation as she spins to face the mirror above the dresser. She cocks her head, examining her reflection.

What are you thinking about, love?

I watch her reflection, completely enraptured, as one of her hands comes up and caresses her own breast. She stares into her own eyes as her fingers tweak and pull at her nipple. Her chest rises and falls in an unsteady rhythm as she works herself up.

"That's it baby," I whisper into the night as if she can hear me. "Touch yourself for me, princess. Make that pussy nice and wet for me."

I feel my own core heat from the sight before me. My little princess is teasing herself while watching her reflection becoming more and more desperate with each touch. Her mouth opens into a rounded shape and I can tell she's moaning in pleasure.

She suddenly stops and moves to lay on the bed. Pulling a laptop towards her, she starts it up. After a moment, the screen illuminates with a video. Squinting in order to make out the small screen, I realize my girl has turned on some porn. Not just any porn either, she's watching a video of some busty blonde eating out the cunt of a petite brunette.

My naughty, naughty girl. How fucking perfect you are.

Scarlett's right hand slides beneath the waistband of her pants. I can't see exactly how she's playing with herself from this angle but I imagine she's rubbing soft circles around her needy nub. *Fuck*! I'd give almost anything to watch her delicate little fingers strumming her clit for me. Her eyes stay locked on the video as her hands work together to play with both her pussy and tits in tandem. My dirty little princess is curious about what it would be like to fuck another girl. *Good.* She clearly was left wanting more after our coffee date earlier. At least, she better be thinking of me while she touches herself.

Her hips buck and her head falls back as her pleasure begins to build. I bite my bottom lip to stifle a moan. She's fucking gorgeous as she humps the air in desperation. Her eyes are now closed as she fucks her own hand. I wonder if she's picturing me while she chases ecstasy.

A sinister sting of jealousy thrums through me. What if she's thinking about someone else?

"*Let's find out,*" he whispers. It'd be wrong though. I

could allow myself to violate her mind and play with her desires, but I shouldn't.

"Then you'd know who she's thinking about while she strums her slick little slit," the demon's voice sing-songs with a sadistic lilt. It's probably a terrible idea to listen to a Hell demon, and yet...

The rhythm of her hands is desperately furious as she seeks her release. She's so close. My own pussy weeps watching her play with herself. I want that hand to be mine. I want to claim her body and soul until she's completely and utterly *mine*. I want each beat of her heart, each breath that inflates her lungs, each and every single thought that runs through her mind, to belong to me.

I want her.

She crashes into her orgasm with such wild ferocity that I can barely stand to watch. And yet, I can't tear my eyes away from her. Her back bows and her head is thrown back as her entire body ripples with sensation. Her cheeks are red and puffy. A single tear rolls down her cheek and I'm absolutely desperate to taste it. She's the most wildly beautiful creature I've ever seen.

She lets out a long sigh and collapses against her bed. We both lie still and silent for a moment. Then she shimmies out of her pants, crawls under her comforter, and shuts off her light.

Time to play princess.

CHAPTER SEVEN

Morgan

Her room smells like her—like caramel and coffee. It's bitter and sweet and absolutely intoxicating. The walls are barren of much and the decor is bland. It's clearly a guest room with very little thought put into the design. I find myself wondering how my girl would decorate. Does she like florals and pastels? Or dark minimalism? I want to know if our styles will clash or be cohesive. I would let her decorate our walls any way she wanted if it meant she'd stay with me forever.

Crawling on top of her sleeping form, I can't help but savor the moment. Even in sleep, the spell she's cast around me pulls me towards her. Her chest rises and falls in a soft and steady rhythm indicating that she's deep asleep. I guess that orgasm tired her out. Too bad I have no intention of letting her mind or body rest right now.

There are things about being a succubus I enjoy. The eternal life, preservation of youth and beauty, are all nice. I could do without the harsh deadline of finding exactly thirteen victims by the blood moon, but so is the price you pay, right? The one thing that I truly love about my deal with the Devil, is the power. I have the power to provoke and control desire, even within dreams. It took a lot of trial and error but my demon and I have a system—I enter their dreams and seduce them, arousing our victims in their sleep, while my demon stays behind, controlling our body and using it to claim our victims souls. The Hell demon inhabiting my soul and I might not always see eye to eye on things, but when it comes to fucking and sucking, we make a great team.

This time we're in complete agreement—no sucking, just fucking. We will claim her body until it's absolutely spent but her soul is safe...*for now.*

Pulling the blanket down ever so gently, I begin to expose her sleeping form. Her pale skin glows in the bright moonlight. Her nipples pebble and tighten as the cool night air hits them. They're begging to be sucked.

Fuck, I want to lick her from head to toe and taste every delectable inch of her.

Pulling the blanket further down, I uncover her bare pussy. She's shaved. Her pretty pale skin glistens with the cum she left for me. My mouth waters and my core heats just being this close to her naked form. But I need to be careful, if she wakes before I'm done with her she'll freak. Can't have her waking up to a naked succubus straddling her, that'd probably not be great for our budding relationship, right?

As gently as I can, I spread her legs open, exposing her beautiful core to me. So pretty and pink. I feel my tongue stretch and my eyes begin to shift as the demon within fights his way to the surface.

"*Patient! I'm going*," I warn him within my mind.

"*She needs our tongue, our fingers. Let me make her come*," he begs me. A hunger I've never heard before placed in his tone.

He's not wrong. Relenting, I slip into the void—the space between conscious thoughts. It's a vast empty space, almost impossible to navigate unless you know what you're doing. Luckily for me, I've had centuries of practice.

Her mind is easy enough to access through the void. It calls to me as if it knows I'm supposed to be there. I'm going to make myself at home in the cobwebs of her mind. Entering her subconscious is like slipping into a warm shower after a cold day–comforting.

We're in a corn maze. *Interesting*. The moon shines high in the sky, illuminating the tall stalks that surround us and scattering distorted shadows across the dirt below. My brow furrows. I can only elicit dreams of desire, not fear. So this dreamscape is confusing. Unless she wants to be afraid.

Does my sweet little princess like fear? *That's very interesting.*

I can play the big bad wolf for my pretty little princess.

I love to play in dreams. Now that I've mastered it, that is. At first it was disarming, but now I'm an expert. Anything I imagine, I can pull from the air. It's a fucking dream after all. With a simple thought I'm able to grab a flashlight from nowhere. *Fucking cool, right?* Pressing the small button embedded in the plastic handle, a bright beam illuminates the path ahead.

I've landed in an empty part of her maze. There's no noise, no people, nothing. And yet, electricity zaps through the air as if at any moment, lightning will flash across the sky. I can taste her as a light breeze blows through my blonde locks. Her fear calls to me, wrapping itself around my senses and luring me towards her.

Scarlett's excited.

She *wants* me to hunt her.

"Come out, come out wherever you are, princess!" I call into the emptiness surrounding me.

Holding the light towards the ground, I slowly wander further into the maze. Clever little prey is hiding nice and quiet.

"If you give yourself up, I'll go easy on you! If you hide from me, I'll drag you out by your hair and force you to your knees!"

My threat does the trick. Light rustling up ahead grabs my attention. She's close. Turning towards the sound, I loudly stalk towards my girl. I want her to hear me. I want her to know I'm coming for her.

I turn a corner and a flash of movement catches my eye. Raven hair dances along the crisp fall air before disappearing around the row of corn. I'm right behind her.

Anticipation thrums heavily through my entire body. I don't just want to catch her. I want to have her, taste her, savor her, claim her. I want to be the first and last girl she *ever* fucks.

Tonight, I get to convince her how good it'll be when she gives herself over to me.

As I round the stalks she just fled behind, I see her running up ahead. She turns her head to glance back at me. She's magnificent. Her cheeks are reddened from cold and exhaustion. Her hair is wild and unkempt. Her darkened pupils are blown wide, reflecting the light of the moon overhead. She slows her pace to take in my appearance. Her eyes glimmer with fearful anticipation, the sight traveling straight to my clit, causing it to throb with need.

Despite the desperate pace at which she's running from me, the magic of this dream world has me gaining on her. My beautiful girl wants me to catch her. She wants me to corrupt her. I'm close enough now to taste her scent on the wind—caramel and coffee but with a hint of something else, something floral. It's intoxicating. I want to savor her taste as I consume the entirety of her pristine flesh with my fucking tongue.

She takes another turn, then another, desperate to lose me. It doesn't work. I'm right on her heels. The light from my flashlight illuminates flashes of her as she desperately tries to escape in the twists and turns of the maze. The anticipation of catching her has my heart pounding and my palms sweating. I grip the flashlight tighter, not wanting it to slip from my hand. She takes a final turn and falters.

She's led us to a clearing. It's a wide open space in the center of the maze. She spins in circles, fearfully looking for an escape route. Her raven locks whip around her face as she spins.

"Nowhere left to run, princess. You're mine now."

I use the flashlight to peruse over her body, taking her in as I slowly approach. She's in a simple black dress that hugs her tight little silhouette snuggly. Her delicate curves are prominently displayed under the tight fabric. Her feet are bare and scratched from our chase. Her pale skin glowing under the light of the high moon. She's so vulnerable.

I cock my head to the side as I approach her. Her fear is pungent. So is her arousal.

"Get on your knees, baby girl. Maybe I'll take it easy on you if you beg me sweetly and lick my cunt thoroughly."

Her eyebrows shoot up at my suggestion but I don't miss how she clenches her thighs. She's as desperate to taste me as I am her. She sways uneasily on her feet. She can't decide if she wants to stay or flee.

Either way, you're mine now, princess.

As I close the final few steps between us, she turns to run but I grab her by the hair and pull. She shrieks as I wrench her back towards me. She stumbles and I wrap an arm around her to hold her up, pulling her back against my front. She squirms against me but I hold her tightly. The more she fights against me the harder my nipples turn. I *crave* her fight.

"Your fear is the sweetest scent I've ever smelled, like blossoming magnolias in the spring," I whisper as I run my nose along the column of her neck, letting her smell completely overwhelm me. She shivers involuntarily, her fight fleetingly lost in the wind as she gives into me.

"Let me go," my sweet girl pleas without any conviction.

She's going to be such a good girl for me.

"I don't think you really want that sweet girl." My hand holding the flashlight trails down her body to the hem of her dress. I let the butt of the plastic handle lightly skim the flesh of her upper thighs, teasing her. Her breathing is ragged as I gently caress her pale skin. My other arm is still banded around her chest, holding her in place. "I think you'd rather have me touch you."

With one hand teasing higher and higher up her thighs, my other hand finds her stiff nipple. I use my thumb and index finger to roll and pull her nipple through the fabric of her tight dress. Her sharp intake of breath quickly turns into a loud moan. She arches her back, begging me to continue.

"Such a desperate slut for me, aren't you?" I move my hand to her other breast, teasing that nipple as well. "I bet your needy little pussy is dripping for me right now isn't it?"

She shakes her head in denial. A single fat tear rolling down her cheek.

I glide the handle of the flashlight higher, letting it skim the apex of her thighs.

Breathing into her neck, I whisper to her, "You're not curious? Don't want to know just how good it can feel to be with a woman?" I rock the flat plastic butt of the flashlight against her pussy lips, eliciting a soft moan from my prey. "See, that's the thing about being with a woman," her hips rock as she begins to chase her own pleasure. "We know how to play with a pussy." I maneuver the torch in my hand so the edge rubs against her clit with just enough pressure. "We know how good it feels to have someone focused entirely on each aching pulse that runs along our folds." Her head falls back against my shoulder as she grinds her hips desperately, finally giving in completely. Her breasts heave as she sucks in desperate breaths. She's a radiant creature.

"Please," she whines as she grinds her ass against me.

"You want me to make you come, little slut?" This is too fun. She's so fucking eager, turned on by the fear and thrill of the chase. Her desperate corruption is a pleasure I intend to savor.

"Yes!"

"Say you're mine," I command with a consuming need to possess her. My fingers flick her nipples, one then the other, making sure they're alert and throbbing.

"I can't—" she moans as I rub furious circles around her cunt. "Kyle…"

His name leaving her lips while I touch her has me seeing red. She needs to learn she's mine. *All fucking mine.* I'm going to kill that asshole and keep her for myself. Even if I have to chain her to a bed and lick her cunt until she's too delirious from pleasure to remember how to even say that motherfucker's name.

What can I say? I'm a jealous fucking bitch when it comes to what's mine.

I rip my hands away from her, shoving her angrily to the ground. She falls to the dirt with a thump. Spinning onto her back, she looks at me incredulously. She's pissed.

Good. I'm pissed too, princess.

Throwing myself on top of her before she can speak, I straddle her at the waist. The flashlight falls to the ground and rolls, illuminating our combined forms in a spotlight of bright light. Her breath hitches as I rock my hips, letting our cunts rub against each other. Wrapping her silky raven locks around my fist, I pull her face to mine. I don't kiss her gently. She had her chance to give in to me, now I'm taking what I want. I plunder her mouth, my tongue attacking hers with obsessive fury. She moans into my mouth as I take everything from her.

My clit pulses with each pounding thump of my heart. My tits are heavy and aching for her sweet little fingers. Her pale and slender digits would look so good palming my heavy breasts. I'm desperate to have her hands caressing me. As much as I love claiming her, I can't wait to teach her how to please me in return.

"Are you going be a good girl and let me fuck you?" I ask as I pull back from our kiss.

She's a breathless mess beneath me. Her lips are red and swollen from our kiss. She looks beautiful in red. Her name suits her perfectly. *My radiant red princess.* I'm going to cover her in scarlett marks and make her come so hard she'll never think about a cock ever again.

"Yes," she whispers on an exhale, giving me the permission I need to take.

Lifting up the hem of her dress fully, I expose her pretty pink pussy. Her wet arousal makes it glisten in the moonlight. She's the embodiment of perfection.

"No panties?" I ask as I trail one long red fingernail across her slick folds, making her shiver. "Such a good little slut for me, aren't you?"

She moans as I trace delicate circles around her clit with my red tipped finger. I rise to my knees and pull up the hem of my skirt, exposing myself to her. Her eyes shoot to my shaved pussy.

"Do you want to touch it?"

She licks her lips, considering. After a moment she nods and reaches a hand out, gently and tentatively letting her fingers glide against my folds. Her touch is the softest little stroke. It sends a shiver shooting down my spine.

"Fuck, princess," I moan as I throw my head back towards the moon above.

I fight the urge to move my hips, allowing her the space to explore. I don't want to rush her. Her fingers slowly pull my folds open, exposing me to her. The cool night air nips at my tender flesh in the most pleasingly uncomfortable way. Her breath quickens as she takes me in, the sweet smell of her fearful arousal intensifying. She trails a single digit through my wetness until she finds my clit. My breasts ache and my walls clench as she rubs small and delicate circles around the tiny bundle of nerves. I'm so grateful that in this dream state I can just be a normal human woman with a normal pussy, no viscous teeth to worry about.

"Does that feel good?" she asks, hesitation laced in her tone. She's so uncertain. I need her to see how fucking sexy and powerful she can be.

"So good, sweet girl. Keep touching me just like that."

My praise seems to work. She rubs me with stronger, more confident, strokes until my pussy drips down my thighs. Heat builds in my core. She feels so good beneath me, exploring me.

I'm never letting you go, you look too perfect between my thighs.

I can feel my orgasm building but it's too soon, I'm not done with her yet. I need her to truly see how good this can be. I need her to submit to me, to give in to me fully. I'm not leaving this dream until she's mine.

I gently remove her hand from between my soaking wet folds. She looks confused, and slightly hurt. *Fuck*. That hurt in her eyes does something to me. "I don't want to come just yet," I reassure her before leaning down to cup her cheek. "I want to play with my girl a little more before I consume you completely." I dive into her mouth. Her lips part, allowing me access. I ravage her mouth with mine. Our tongues stroke each other in an intimate dance. She tastes like my sweetest little treat.

"Fuck, princess, you're going to ruin me," I growl as I trail kisses down her throat. She's a moaning mess beneath me. "You make me crazy." I suck and nip at her neck, leaving marks all across her skin. I want her marked as mine, even if it's only for right now and here. Tomorrow she'll wake and think this was all just a creation of her subconscious. But, if I play my cards right, I'll convince her she needs to turn her dreams into reality.

"Say you're mine, pretty girl," I mumble against her breast before biting down into her pale flesh. She screams out as my teeth sink far enough to draw blood.

The metallic taste of her blood fills my mouth. I lap at it greedily, spreading the crimson all over her sensitive nipple. Her shrieks of pain turn into moans as I use my tongue to flick her stiffening tit.

"Say it," I demand of her as I rise. Her blood stains my teeth and feral need swirls through my eyes as I stare down at her.

"Wh—What?"

"Say you're mine and I'll let you come." I rub her pussy with my fingers and her back arches off the ground. She's absolutely drenched for me.

I throw her leg over my hip and drag her towards me, angling us so our dripping cores are lined up perfectly.

"Please," my sweet little seductress pleads.

"You beg so pretty, princess," I coo before I begin to move.

I grind my hips against hers. Pinning her to the ground with my hand against her throat, I watch as her pupils dilate. Slotting her as tightly against me as I can and holding her thigh up with my other hand, I lock our cores together, her slickness melding with mine.

We fit together perfectly.

"You want me to fuck this pretty little pussy? Say it!" I punctuate the final words with another roll of my hips. Our clits rub against each other, the friction is exquisite. Her raging pulse thunders against my palm. We align like two pieces of a complex puzzle. She was fucking made for me.

She shakes her head as she pants and moans. A deplorable idea crosses my mind. It's oh so wicked. Just the thought has desire rushing through me like wildfire. Removing my hand from her throat, I pull a long hunting knife from the air. Her eyes widen in horror. The sweet stench of magnolias swirls around me. She tries to squirm away but my fingers dig into her tender flesh holding her steady, fucking her pussy against mine. Her fear, her lust, her perky little tits, her heat against mine is almost too good—I feel my climax beginning to rise.

"If you won't say it, then I'll have to make sure I claim you in a way you'll never forget."

Our swollen buds slide against eachother again and again as I fuck her into the dirt. She can't stop the moan falling from her lips as I promise her the dangerous pleasure she craves. Her hips move against mine in a frantic motion as she chases her release. Each roll of her hips causes her bleeding breasts to bounce up and down in rhythm with my own. She's a fucking masterpiece. I'm never letting her go.

Her pace turns quicker, her hips thrusting against mine as she edges closer and closer to ecstasy. Bringing the blade down to her exposed stomach I slice at her skin. She shrieks in pain and jumps. However, the frantic movement causes her pussy to grind violently against mine. She can't help the moan of pleasure that follows the pained cry.

I carve at her skin. Holding her leg tightly in one hand to keep her where I want her, and holding the blade I'm using to carve her up in the other hand, I fuck her. Blood trails down her stomach towards the space between us. Dark red warmth seeps down her form to where we are combined, adding to the slickness of our desire. The flashlight illuminates her form beneath me. Her bloodied breasts bounce as I fuck her with wild abandon. She's a fucking masterpiece and there's no way she's escaping my clutches now. I need more of her blood, more of her pleasure, more of *her*.

"Please, please…" my sweet girl begs.

"Almost done carving you up babe, hold on a minute longer, then you can come with me."

She whines at me but complies, biting her plump bottom lip in her teeth to avoid falling without permission. I fuck her and slice her simultaneously. Each slick thrust of her pussy against mine has me moving closer and closer to release. I carve the symbol of my demon into her skin with frantic strokes, blood coating where we're joined.

"Fuck, babe," I grunt as I harshly grind my clit against hers and throw the knife to the ground. She's carved up with my mark. *Mine*. It's scraped into her fucking flesh. She. Is. Mine.

"Come for me, princess. I want to feel you come against me."

My good girl obeys immediately, throwing her head

back and tensing as every nerve ending in her body fires with pleasure. I feel her swollen folds spasm as her orgasm crashes violently. Her dark hair splayed on the ground beneath her, her pale skin bloodied, her sweet scent invading my soul. It's fucking perfection. *She* is perfection. I want to tear her wide open, feasting on her fear and pleasure as if it's my last fucking meal.

Watching her come is enough to push me over the edge with her. Wave after wave of pleasure rips through me. The orgasm has me screaming out into the cool autumn air. My entire core pulses desperately as the orgasm rushes through me. It's the hardest I've come in as long as I can remember. Maybe it's the magic of the dream. Or maybe it's just her.

Silence engulfs us as we both come back down. The only sounds are the soft rustle of the stalks surrounding us swaying in the breeze and our ragged breathing. I finally open my eyes and shift my heavy lidded gaze to the woman below me. Her chest heaves as she tries to calm her body. She's a mess—covered in dirt and blood and our combined cum. I scan every inch of her body, entranced with how magnificent she is.

Grabbing the bloodied knife from the ground, I bring the blade up in front of my face. I let my tongue glide through the sticky sweet blood along the knife's edge. Scarlett's eyes widen in horror and lust. Her blood is sweet and metallic in my mouth. I close my eyes and moan as her taste covers my tongue.

When I open my eyes, I'm thrown back. I'm back in my body, back in her room, back to reality.

My girl lays peacefully beneath me, breathing softly against her pillow. I pull my fingers from her tight little cunt, the orgasm I gifted her in her dream and in real life, now passed. The dream is done. I can't help the slight sting of disappointment at seeing her not covered in the marks of our violent pleasure. I knew my carving only existed within the dream, and yet, something in my chest aches as I see her without my symbol etched into her pale flesh. Back in reality her pristine skin is spotless, free of my mark.

"Not our soul to claim for Hell, yet." His voice is back in my mind, slithering across our shared cognition.

Her phone suddenly illuminates on the nightstand beside us pulling my attention away from the sleeping form below me.

KYLE: Landlord says the window's fixed. We can move back in tomorrow.

I know what I *should* do. I *should* text him from her phone and ask him to meet up. I *should* go to where he agrees to meet and seduce him. I *should* ride his cock until he's a weak mess then unleash my teeth and suck him dry. I *should* consume his soul, get my thirteenth victim and flee.

I should do all of that. But I don't.

The thought of leaving her is too painful. I need to find a way to get the soul I need and keep her. I might be being selfish but I refuse to give her up. I'll just have to think of a plan.

So instead, I delete the message. Over my dead fucking body will she be moving back in with him. She's mine. It may have been just a dream to her, but not to me. She won't share her bed or body with anyone besides me from here on out.

Replacing her phone on the nightstand, I stand and adjust my clothes back into place. My girl looks so peaceful now that I've fucked her into utter exhaustion. Good. She needs some rest for what I have in store for her.

I sneak quietly from the house. Making sure the door is locked and secure as I go. Before heading back to my hotel, I pop open the passenger door to her car. I will be getting her a much nicer and more secure vehicle soon. My princess will not be driving around in this hunk of junk for much longer. Retrieving the pretty package from my bag, I place it gently on the seat of her car. Before closing the door, I make sure the card is securely on top where she can easily see it.

Looking back up to the quiet townhouse I can't help but smile.

See you soon, princess.

CHAPTER EIGHT

Scarlett

The fall air is crisp and fresh as I suck it down into my lungs in an attempt to slow my heartbeat. The front of me is exposed—very exposed—showing way more skin than I'm used to. The thick, red cape hangs from my shoulders straight down to the ground, keeping at least the back of me warm. A cold breeze brushes over the areas of my exposed flesh, leaving a ripple of goosebumps in its path. I can't fucking believe I'm doing this. A shiver runs down my spine as I keep walking. I'd like to think it's just from the cold, but part of me knows it's from the anticipation of what's to come.

I can't fucking believe I'm doing this.

I found a box on the passenger seat of my car this morning. Inside was the same Little Red Riding Hood costume I'd coveted at the costume shop and a note. It didn't say who the gift was from, it simply read:

Hell House

7 P.M.

Wear this and nothing else.

The note didn't need to be signed. I knew it was her—Morgan. Somehow I just knew in my bones that she left it for me. I should be horrified that this woman seems to be stalking me and breaking into my car to leave me presents…but I'm not. I should have called the cops or at least told Kyle and let him deal with it. But instead, I put on the costume and parked outside the haunted house on the outskirts of town at exactly 6:55. I can't believe I didn't even put on underwear. I know it's what the note implied, but still, I've never walked around bare like this before in my life. I'm just not that kind of girl. Rubbing my thighs together, I can't help but feel exposed and slightly aroused by the fact that anyone could lift up my skimpy little dress and see all of me. *I'm both horrified and turned on by this new version of myself.*

Part of me knows that I shouldn't have come tonight but I can't shake Morgan from my mind; especially after the dream I had about her last night. I woke up covered in my own cum. I didn't think that was even possible for women to do in their sleep. I thought it was just a teenage boy thing. Shame rocked through me when I realized why I'd woken up damp and sticky. I'd hurriedly stuffed my soiled sheets in Sam's washer and practically ran to shower.

There was also a part of me that was strangely disappointed to see my perfectly normal stomach. It was completely clear of any marks as I looked into the bathroom mirror and undressed to shower away the evidence of my naughty dream. Deep down, my fucked up subconscious wished she had actually carved me up while fucking me. Evidently my mind wants this woman—*badly*. So, against my better judgment, I'm here.

Hell House looms dauntingly in front of me. Gray clouds infused with the last burning embers of sunlight frame the building, giving it an ethereal glow. Screams of horror emanate from within. From the outside it simply looks like one of those old mansions that once housed some well-off family, but has since fallen into disrepair. Once a year however, it is transformed into a haunted house known across the country for its over-the-top stunts. The liability waiver that guests are required to sign before entering went viral a few years back and that only helped to make the place even more packed. I've never been here before because I've always been too scared.

But I'm sick of being scared.

I approach two very large men who are dressed as some type of demons guarding the front door and my heart rate kicks up. A nervous lump of anxiety forms in my throat and

I try my best to take a few deep breaths and calm myself.

They're just people, just like me, in costumes. No one can really hurt me inside a haunted house, right? This is just for fun.

Peeking through the slightly open door behind the bouncers, strobe lights flash and illuminate nothing but dark smoke. A woman's scream rings out, causing me to jump. Fear flows through my veins like fire, whispering for me to turn around and head back to my apartment to wait for Kyle to come home, just like I usually would be doing on a Friday night. But some unseen force propels me forward and I continue up the steps towards the door.

"Did you sign the waiver online?" one of the demons at the entrance asks while inclining his head slightly to the side. The sinister look of his mask doesn't fit with his down to business tone. Everything about this place is unsettling and yet, the fear and anxiety is doing something to my body that I've never felt before. It's as if everything is too hot, too tight, too much, and yet I don't want it to stop.

"Yes," I manage to squeak out between stuttering breaths.

They check my name on their computer to confirm I filled out all the paperwork before placing a stamp on my hand.

"Welcome to Hell," the second man says, swinging his arm towards the open door and granting me entrance. There's a hint of laughter in his voice and I'm certain he thinks I'll be running out of here crying in exactly five minutes. He might be right.

The main door leads to a darkened and eerily silent main hallway. On either side is a series of baroque ornate doors, all closed. There's smoke pooling around my ankles and white strobes flashing all around me. Deafening silence surrounds me. I try my best to acclimate to the darkness. My heart pounds, my breathing is ragged and rapid; anxiety is twisting my insides like constricting snakes. My body is screaming for me to get out of here but I can't. I can't explain it but I know she's here. I know she's behind one of these doors waiting for me. My goddess is waiting to play with me, and that thought has desire leaking down my thighs.

A bang against one of the doors to my left shatters the silence, causing me to leap to the right. My hands fly to my chest and I stumble backwards. My back falls against a door and it flies open. I fall backwards through the doorway and into another world entirely.

Turning on my heels, I take in my surroundings. It's empty in here but not silent. There's shrieks and screams of terror being pushed out of speakers. It's still dark and smoky in here but everything has a blue tinge to it. Jagged shards of mirrors line the walls in awkward angles.

Moving closer to one of the shards, I notice it's one of those strange mirrors that distorts everything. My face is unrecognizable in it. My reflected self looks terrified but thrilled to be in a sexy costume alone in a haunted house. My black hair is braided into two long strands that fall out from the hood of my cape and frame my small chest nicely. The tight, white, corset style bodice of the dress accentuates my curves, while the short green skirt flows out from my waist making my hips appear round and full. My lips are painted a shade of red to match the cape around me. I completed the look with thigh high black boots that have a chunky heel. The reflection is a version of me I've always wanted to see but have never been brave enough to pursue—not until now. *Not until her.* I like this version of me reflecting back through these creepy-ass mirrors.

The exit suddenly slams shut behind me with a loud crack. I spin rapidly, flinging my head back and forth, the cape whipping around my body, as I search for the person who slammed the door. But there's no one there. All I see is the thousands of distorted images of myself, grotesque figures that are me and yet not, their eyes piercing me with a fearful gaze. No one else is here.

This place is too creepy. I need to find Morgan and get out of here.

Where the hell is everyone?

Stepping further into the room, I notice that it seems to narrow into a mirrored hallway. A hall of mirrors. *Shit.* I step closer and closer, biting my bottom lip until the metallic taste of blood floods my tastebuds. The hallway in front of me is completely mirrored; blue and purple strobe lights flash on and off, causing a refracted light effect and distorting the length of the hallway. I can't tell where it ends. I move forward, watching off to the side as hundreds of me move forward in sync with my motions.

Movement at the other end of the hallway catches my attention, drawing my eyes upward. A figure stands at the far end of the mirrored tunnel. She strides right into my line of sight, her hypnotic blue eyes staring straight at me. Morgan is wearing a skin tight skeleton suit which hugs her delicious figure tightly. To match, her face is decorated like a sugar skull mask. Black and white paint contours her features; crimson sequins rim her eyes, glimmering in the strobe lights. The sight of her causes my mouth to go dry and my pussy to pulse with desire. Her tits bob and sway as she saunters closer to me. She's definitely wearing nothing underneath her skin tight bodysuit as the hardened peaks of her nipples grab my attention. I rub my legs together to try and elevate the throbbing between my thighs.

"Hello princess," she purrs at me from across the hall of smoke and mirrors separating us. "I'm so very glad you came." Her voice is smooth and sweet like honey.

"I knew it was you." Is all I can manage to say as she transfixes me with her gaze.

"Of course it was me. It will *always* be me. You're mine and I absolutely do not share. If someone else were to request that you meet up with them without any underwear on, I'd be forced to disembowel them and shove their innards down their throat." She steps closer, making my breath stutter against the confines of my chest.

Who the fuck says things like that?

But I can't deny the way she makes me feel. She steals the air from my lungs, hell, from the entire room. It's like everything else ceases to exist when she's around. As she gets closer to me her scent wraps around me, the magical mix of vanilla and jasmine that she seems to emanate. I want to taste it, I want to taste *her*.

"I'm yours?" I ask. Her lips tip into a devious smile as possessive fire rages in her eyes.

"Of course you're mine, princess. Don't you feel it? This pull between us? Fate has brought you to me." She steps into my space, the warmth of her making me practically melt where I stand. Her hand reaches out to push the hood from my head, her hand trailing down the length of my braided pigtail. "And tonight I'm going to ruin you."

Her words are wicked and cause my stomach to flutter in anticipation. "Ruin me?"

"Uh-huh." Her hand tightens on my braid as she pulls, dragging me against her. She's so soft and warm; my body immediately responds to her touch. Having our skin this close, our breasts pushing together, makes me completely desperate for her to touch me, kiss me, *take* me. Her hardened nipples skim against mine, teasing me in the most unbearable way. "You, my love, are dressed as a sweet little good girl, so clearly you're the hunted," she pulls my hair again, making my scalp tingle. "And I'm the hunter."

Her lips brush across mine in a seductive dance. "I'm going to fucking *ruin* you."

Her words cause my mouth to fall open in a gasp. She takes the opportunity to press her lips harshly against mine, her tongue quickly driving into my open mouth. She strikes like a viper, attacking me with such passion that I nearly fall backwards. Her tongue fights against mine, her lips pulsing and urging me to reciprocate. I can't help but give in. I kiss her back, allowing my lips to move against hers, and my tongue to join her dance. I've never been kissed like this, with such need. Her kiss is aggressive and desperate. Her hands fall to my waist as she grinds my body against hers, eliciting a hungered groan from me. She smiles against my mouth, happy with the animalistic noises she's pulling from me. Without being consciously aware of what my body is doing, I roll my hips, pushing my pussy into hers. She pulls back slightly and flashes a wicked smile at me as she stares down at me through hooded lids, her eyes laced with lust and desire.

"So fucking needy for me, aren't you princess?" Her thumb glides across my bottom lip, hooking on the cut I made earlier and opening it again. I hiss at the pain. Everything about this is so similar to my dream, as if she knows my subconscious desires and has planned out how to bring them to life. The thought is unsettling. Perhaps she has snaked her way inside me and knows exactly what I want, what I need.

She pulls herself from me, examining my blood on the pad of her thumb. Without hesitation she brings the digit to her mouth, sucking me from her finger with a growl. "Mine," her voice is low and possessive; her eyes darkening in a way that should scare me, but the need I have for her is too powerful, too potent, too blinding. I want her to take every last piece of me, consume me completely and leave nothing behind. I want to be *hers*.

"Yours," I nod in agreement.

Stepping into me yet again she grabs my hips fiercely, slamming my core against hers as she grinds against me. I moan in delight, not even caring if others walk in and see us essentially dry humping in public. She leans her head down to my neck and brings her lips to the juncture of my shoulder. She bites down, hard. I scream out but her hands around my hips hold me firm, moving me to continue writhing against her. Each roll of my hips against her brings pulsing pleasure to my core. She feels so good. Her bite turns to a bruising kiss, replacing the pain with intense pleasure. I moan loudly as desire courses through me. Her lips release my tender flesh and her mouth moves up the column of my neck, kissing, licking, and driving me wild. My clit is throbbing angrily. Fuck, I might come before we even get our clothes off. I've never been this worked up before. I'm used to being there for someone else's release. I've never had someone work me up solely for my pleasure. It's maddening and wonderful.

When her lips reach my ear she pauses. "You're going to run, Scarlett," she whispers. I can feel my need for her building, heat moving through my core as I continue to shamelessly grind against her. "And I'm going to chase you. When I catch you, I'm going to strip you naked, tie you up, and claim that pretty little pussy until you scream my name loud enough that everyone on Hell and Earth knows exactly who you belong to."

I pause at her insinuation. This is fun and all but she can't be serious. There are other people around. Plus, I don't even know her last name or anything about her. I'm not about to let some stranger fuck me in a haunted house while others watch. I'm not that type of girl. *Right?*

"Wha—what about the other people here? What if we get caught? They'll throw us out." I try to step back away from her but she holds me tightly against her.

"There's no one else here. I rented out the entire place. As soon as you entered, the crew cleared out everyone. It's just you and me in here, sweet girl."

I try to wrap my mind around what she's saying. It can't be true, can it? To rent this place out would cost a fortune. But she's right, I haven't seen or heard anyone else since I got here. Maybe we truly are alone.

As if she can feel my unease she quickly reassures me. "Princess," she pulls back, tilting my head up so that our eyes meet. "I mean it. You're mine and I'm not sharing you with anyone. If anyone's eyes dared to look at you while you came I'd pluck their eyeballs from their sockets, throw them to the dirt beneath our feet, and pop them with the heel of my stilettos. The only one looking at you, touching you, tasting you," she punctures each word with a kiss to my neck, causing desire to fill me yet again, "will be me."

"And if you don't catch me?" I ask, secretly hoping the answer still results in her touching me more.

A sinister smirk pulls at her lips. "I will catch you princess and when I do, I will make damn sure you never question the lengths to which I will go to have you ever again." Her words are laced with a potent combination of threat and lust, making my skin tingle and my pussy clench. "Now *run*."

CHAPTER NINE

Morgan

Scarlett is such a good girl for me, running just as I instructed her to do. I knew after her dream last night I had to make her dark fantasies come true. I had to turn her desires into reality and show her just how good I can make her feel. I know that I should be hunting my thirteenth victim, but hunting her is so much more fun. Plus, I still have a few more days left until the blood moon.

The long red cape flies behind her as she spins and hurtles back through the room of mirrors. When she reaches the other side of the room, she turns back to me, fear filling those beautiful doe eyes. I give her a wicked smile, letting her know I fully intend on hunting her down and taking her. She squeals, the sound traveling straight to my cunt, before she hurls the heavy door open and disappears into the hallway.

Her innocent fear is absolutely addictive. I've been hunting men for so long—too long. They're all cocky bastards until they feel my barbs sinking into their precious flesh as my demon teeth rip them apart. Only then do I get their fear. It's delicious but brief. My princess, on the other hand, is a buffet of sweet fear. Every single breath she's taken since entering this building has called to the monster inside me, feeding its unquenchable need for terror and pain. It's intoxicating. I'm high as fuck on the addictive taste of her horror and desire. And then there's her blood. *Fuck!* The taste of her blood was enough to drive me completely fucking feral. My pussy is weeping with need for this girl and I've barely kissed her tonight. I want to cut her open and use her blood as lube to fuck both her tight little holes while she screams for me. The delicious idea has my core heating. I've never felt such a strong pull toward another creature and I can't even suck from her, this is purely for pleasure. And *her pleasure* is exactly what's on the menu tonight.

Having given her enough of a head start, I begin stalking my way after her. She thinks I'm just a human woman, she has no idea that the beast within me is acutely aware of her every move. Her unique scent—the addicting smell of coffee and caramel—lingers in the air behind her. It provides me with a map to follow her every move. My heightened senses are supposed to help me track ideal victims, but right now, I'm using them to hunt down and take my girl. By the end of tonight, she'll never even think about letting anyone else touch her ever again. Fuck Kyle and his average dick that he doesn't even know how to use right. I'll make sure that she comes to me and only me for all her pleasure from now until the end of eternity.

She'll be mine, all fucking mine.

"Oh princess," I shout into the darkness as I enter the main hallway again. "Come out, come out wherever you are."

Nothing. She wants to play. She's so fucking perfect.

"What a naughty girl you are hiding from me, princess," her scent lingers further down the hallway, away from the door we came from. "Maybe I'll punish you when I catch you, spank that pale little ass until you're red and ready for me." The thought of her perfectly pale skin blooming red for me makes my nipples harden against my bodysuit. I can almost taste how sweet her pain will be.

The white strobe lights flash without pattern, clearly meant to disorient patrons. Lucky for me, everything about me changed when I sold my soul to the Devil in exchange for revenge on the man who wronged me, including my eyesight. I see much better in the dark now. I may have a Hellish demon monster where my soul once was, but my heightened senses are a plus.

There are three doors left in the hallway, one to the right, one to the left, and one straight ahead. Her scent is heavy here, coffee and caramel lingers in the air so thick I can almost taste it. I'm so wet for her that my bodysuit is dampening between my thick thighs.

"I know you're down here, Scarlett. I'm going to find you and when I do I'm going to fuck that pretty pussy so hard you'll beg me to stop. I'm going to make you come over and over again until you don't think you can take it anymore. Are you ready to come out now and be my good little fuck doll?"

To the left, a thundering heartbeat catches my attention. She must be over here. My words must be affecting her. *Good.* I want her all worked up and spun so tight she's barely holding on by the time I find her. I'm going to fully corrupt her and claim her. She's mine. Her fear, her pain, her sweetness, her pleasure. All fucking mine.

"Oh Scarlett," I singsong as I swing the door open. It cracks loudly against the wall behind it while I call out for her again. "Come out, come out sweet girl."

This room is different. There's no strobing lights or smoke in this space. It's a wide, empty room filled with oppressive darkness. Red light spills across the space from hanging lanterns above. Blood-red glass hangs between rectangular, black metal lanterns. Each lantern is strung up from matching black chains; the links of metal quietly clinking in the silence. It's as beautiful as it is eerie. As the lanterns swing, they illuminate red dripping down the walls, a clear attempt to get people to believe the walls are bleeding.

If it was blood, this room would smell like iron and rot. It's not blood, it's fucking corn syrup.

Fitting that my Scarlett girl would hide herself in the red room. Scanning the surroundings I see nothing she could be hiding in or under. The room appears completely empty but I know she's here. Her soul is calling to mine.

"I'm going to count down from ten," I can smell her and sense her in here, she's definitely close. "If you come out willingly before then I'll take it easy on you, if not, then I'll eat you whole my little red lovely."

Not a peep.

"Ten…" My eyes scan the darkness for any sign of her.

"Nine…" I move carefully towards the perimeter of the room, following the path of the wall.

"Eight…" Her smell is getting stronger, I must be nearly on top of her. *Where the fuck is she?*

"Seven..." Up ahead there is something strange with the wall.

"Six…" The darkness seems to be hiding something in the back corner. A false half-wall of some kind, hidden in the shadows for actors to hide behind.

"Five…"

Movement across the room catches my attention. Sneaky girl. It's like she was there then gone, hidden behind another half-wall perhaps?

"Four…" I storm across the room. My steps now laced

with purpose as I get closer to my prey.

"Three…" Her scent is even thicker here, as if I'm surrounded by her sweetness. My pussy throbs in anticipation of having her at my mercy.

"Two…" My fingers itch to grab her. The things I want to do to this girl are downright filthy. By the time I'm through with her, no other monster or man will ever be able to fulfill her needs.

Rounding the nearly invisible black frame of the half-wall, I can tell there's a small alcove cut into the wall behind it. A small hiding spot to allow the illusion of monsters appearing out of the darkness. The only monster here tonight though, is me. Crouched down in the empty space, small and vulnerable as a tiny mouse, is my prey. The red cloak wrapped around her shoulders as she shakes with fear. *Fuck,* that fear is intoxicating. The beast within me howls to be unleashed on this precious little creature beneath us.

"One."

Her shimmering eyes flash to me. Her pupils are blown wide, fear swirling through the darkened orbs like smoke.

"Caught you, princess."

She moves so fast I nearly miss her. She attempts to flee, flinging herself out of the alcove and towards the open expanse of the red room. She's quick and nimble, but I'm a demon from Hell that has thousands of years on her. She's no match for me. I grab her around the back of her neck with a single hand and rip her backwards, pulling her back against my front. The subtle swell of her sweet little ass fits perfectly against my thick thighs. I have the sudden urge to bend her over and use my two hands to fuck both her tight little holes until she screams my name so loudly that the Devil himself knows she belongs to me. But I need to ease her into it. She's sweet and delicate and will be so easy to break. I need to go slowly and take my time; savoring each second of her pleasure and every ounce of her pain. I intend to steal everything from her for my selfish gain. And we have all night to make that happen.

Pushing her to the center of the room, I use my free hand to untie her cloak. She shivers at the loss of the warm blanket of velvet. The sound of ripping fabric bounces through the empty cavern of the large room. She jumps at the sudden noise and spins her head to look at me as I rip the red fabric into several long strips.

"Uh-uh, princess," I shake my head at her. "Eyes forward, hands behind your back."

She complies instantly and shivers wrack through my entire being. Her submissive nature is so fucking perfect.

"Good girl," I croon into her ear as I move towards her. I can feel the furious beating of her heart and the quickening of her breath.

Without warning, I tear the flimsy little costume from her body. The cheap fabric easily slips off her slender form and pools at her feet.

"What the hell?" she shrieks, her hands grasping to cover herself.

Now that just won't do.

My hand shoots forward, landing a swift slap to the tender flesh of her ass. She shrieks again and the sound travels straight to my cunt. It's weeping, absolutely desperate for her.

"Hands behind your back and eyes forward princess, I don't like repeating myself."

With an audible breath she complies, placing her hands behind her back. They rest against the red imprint of my hand that now marks her pale and pristine flesh. The sight of my mark on her has the beast within me clawing to get out, craving to claim every inch of her so everyone who looks at her knows exactly who the fuck she belongs to.

Swiftly, I move to bind her hands together with some of the red fabric from her cloak. She winces when I tighten the knot but doesn't pull away, letting me play with her however I want.

"Look at you, princess." I move to circle her slowly and take her in. My finger trails gently across her skin as I stalk around her, taking in the sight before me. "All tied up for me with a big red bow. My perfect present."

When I reach the front of her, I take a moment to savor the sight of her. The way her hands are bound pushes her perfect, perky tits out and up. Her nipples stiff and hard, begging for my touch. I let my eyes wander down her lean figure. I gaze across the flat expanse of her slender stomach, the slight curve of her delicate hips, and down to her perfectly bare pussy. She stands completely vulnerable before me besides her thigh-high boots. She's a fucking vision and I'm nearly breathless wondering how a demon like me has been blessed with a gift so innocent and perfect as her.

"So fucking beautiful." I let her know how much I appreciate her before lowering my head, flicking out my tongue, and tracing slow circles around one of the hardened buds of her breasts. She responds immediately to me, moaning and arching into me. I want so badly to dive in and feast on her but I don't give in to her neediness. I want to play with her first.

"You're so perfect, princess. My beautiful, sexy, smart girl." I let the words sink in, the praise warming her before I move to her other breast and circle that nub with my tongue. Her skin pebbles under my slow strokes and her groans of need fill the air. I want to make her feel so fucking good.

"No," she huffs out between moans. "I'm none of those things," she chokes out as I flick her achingly hard nipple again and again with my tongue, driving her hips to buck in desperation.

Her denial angers me. She should know how fucking amazing she is. She should never doubt what an absolute fucking wonder she is. Grabbing her hips to hold her in place, I move to the tender flesh of her upper breast and bite hard. She screams and tries to back away but I hold her tightly to me. I sink my teeth in further until the snap of skin breaking and the metallic taste of her blood fills my mouth. It reminds me of our shared dream. I hum against her skin in pleasure, fully enjoying turning her dirty dreams into reality. Releasing her skin, I heal the hurt with long licks of my flattened tongue.

"Don't talk down about yourself to me, sweet girl," I speak against the bloodied skin of her breast. Scarlett begins to whine and moan again as I lick and kiss and nip at the entire expanse of her tenderized flesh. "You're perfection and anyone who's ever made you feel less than that will suffer."

I realize I must look like a monster. Rivulets of her blood drip from the corner of my mouth, staining my teeth and lips. I'm threatening people while driving her to insanity with a potent mix of pain and pleasure. I can feel the beast's presence right beneath the surface of my skin. I'm sure that if she looked in my eyes right now, they'd be blood red.

But I can't stop myself. I don't just want her pleasure—*I need it.* She's like a fucking drug soaring through my veins. I place one of her hardened nipples into my mouth and suck hard while flicking with my tongue rapidly against the erect peak, driving her absolutely insane. I so badly want to bite her again, drink down her blood, and hear her shrieks of pain. But I need to take it slowly. I can't scare her away. *Not yet.*

"Please, please," she moans at me.

"Please what, my love?" I tease as I move to the other side, giving her other breast the same treatment.

"Please touch me."

A wicked smirk curls around my lips as I release her tit from my mouth with a pop. "I am touching you, silly."

My fingers gently caress up and down her sides, never touching where she needs me most. I kiss my way up from her chest to her neck. She's already got one large hickey from me but she could use a few more. I suck and lick my way up the column of her neck until she's a complete mess.

She's desperate for me now. Exactly how I need her.

"Do you trust me?" I ask before kissing her lips softly. Her lips are plump and juicy and oh so sweet.

I pull back to look into her eyes. I need her to say yes to this, to agree to my depravity, and submit to me before I take from her what I need. She studies me, her eyes scanning my face for a beat before answering.

"Yes. I trust you. I want to be yours."

Oh sweet girl, you have no idea what you just agreed to.

CHAPTER TEN

Scarlett

The metal chains of the lanterns above us are the only sound in the room. The red glow from them makes Morgan look otherworldly, like a beast sent to consume and destroy. My ragged breathing causes my battered breasts to heave up and down. They're covered in bite marks and hickeys. A small trail of crimson seeps from the bite mark she left, down the curve of my breast and onto my stomach. If this was anyone else I'd be horrified, but I wasn't lying, I trust her. I want her. *I crave her.*

Moving behind me, Morgan disappears. I don't dare turn around but I hear her ripping more fabric from my cape and shuffling around. As much as that spank she gave me earlier had my pussy clenching, I don't want to be punished anymore. When she called me her good girl it did things to me. I think

I'd do pretty much anything to hear those words again.

Suddenly she steps into me, her front against my back. Her warm heat and softness of her form embrace the back of me. Her soft and silky hair tickles the tender skin of my neck as she leans into me. Her arms wrap around me possessively. One traces light circles on the skin of my stomach, just barely above where I need her most, the other paws at my aching breast. I whimper desperately, eliciting an amused laugh from her. Her thumb and pointer finger roll my tender nipple, pinching and pulling it until I'm an absolute puddle. I shamelessly grind my ass into her, desperate for more.

"Say it again," she whispers into my ear. Her tongue traces the shell of it, sending a shiver running down my spine and straight to my clit.

I've never been touched and teased like this. This level of pleasured torture coursing through every nerve in my body is completely foreign. I've never wanted anything—anyone— this badly in my life. I've never felt this wanted either. I'd do anything, give anything, for more of this feeling.

"I trust you. I want you. Please."

The growl that emanates from the woman behind me is feral, animalistic. It's fucking hot as hell.

Her hands leave me and I feel cold at the loss. I never want her to stop touching me.

A moment later her touch returns, but to my head. It

feels as if she's standing behind me and placing a crown on my head. It's a silly, fleeting thought. But she does make me feel special, regal, powerful. She makes me feel awake and alive for the first time in a really long time. She loops something over my head and down my face. As it crosses over my eyes I realize it's torn pieces of my cloak. She keeps moving it down, past my mouth and chin, to my neck. She rests it against the smooth column of my throat before pulling something behind me. The constricting feeling around my neck sends panic coursing through me. I try to bring my arms up to pull the fabric away but they're still bound behind me. I begin the flail and thrust in a desperate attempt to get free but it's no use, I'm caught in her trap.

"Shh. Shh," she placates into my ear. "Relax babe. It's just us. You and me. Let me play with you." One of her hands snakes around my center, tracing a slow path down to between my thighs. "Let me make you feel good."

Her fingers slide down to the lips that lie between my legs. She strokes the outside of my pussy back and forth several times. It feels so good, her delicate and skilled fingers playing me just right. Kyle has only ever touched me in order to pull me open enough to shove his dick inside. No one has ever touched me like this. Her pointer finger and ring finger work together to spread me open, before she uses her middle finger to rub gentle, teasing circles against my clit.

"So wet for me, princess," she whispers as she continues

to touch me. Her warm breath skates across the nape of my neck, eliciting a shiver down my spine. "Are you going to be my good girl and let me do what I want to you?"

Without warning, her finger shoves inside me. I cry out at the sudden intrusion but when her finger starts pumping in and out of my dripping wet pussy, I can't help but relax into the pleasure she's pulling from me.

"Yes! Yes!" I yell as she shoves a second finger into me and curls them at an angle that sets my entire core on fire. Her thumb moves to circle my clit and I can feel the orgasm rushing to me like a wave about to crash down on me, crushing me and stealing my breath.

As suddenly as she entered me, she pulls out. I sag and whine at the sudden loss of her.

"Not yet, princess. You'll come when I say you can." She moves around me again, the end of the red fabric rope she's made sitting in her hand.

Her words shouldn't make my pussy pulse the way it does but there's something so freeing about her taking complete control of me.

She stares at me for a beat, fully taking me in before throwing the other end of the fabric up. I tilt my head back, watching as the end not currently tied around my neck hooks over one of the chains on the ceiling. The metal chain is hung down in a low curve between two metal hooks that connect the chain to lanterns. The red fabric flutters back down from the ceiling, floating like a falling leaf back into her hand.

I'm so fucked.

Sinking to her knees in front of me, Morgan holds the end of my beautiful leash in one hand while the other hand trails up the length of my bare thigh. Her fingers skim the swollen and tender flesh of my clit once again, causing me to writhe and groan. But as I do, her other hand pulls the rope tight, cutting off my air. I scamper to my tippy toes, desperate to avoid being strangled, but it's no use. Panic floods my being as I realize I can barely breathe. My erratic heartbeat thumps widely in my ears. I look down at her in disbelief. But when our eyes meet I realize hers aren't shimmering with anger or malice, they're filled with lust.

She looks away and I follow the path of her gaze with my eyes. She's focused completely on the way her fingers are pumping in and out of me. And then I realize my body is pulsing with more than just fear. Waves of pleasure are radiating from my core. Each push and pull of her fingers drives me closer and closer towards a dive into ecstasy. I never want to breathe again if it feels this good. I want to moan and scream as she curls her fingers and strokes a part of me that has flames of pleasure spreading through my entire being, but the restraint is too tight around my throat. Just as I'm about to fall, she removes her fingers again. The tension around my neck recedes and my feet fall back firmly on the ground.

I gasp for air, desperate to fill my aching lungs. Looking down, I watch as Morgan holds her fingers up to the light. Her fingers glisten in the blood-red light with the evidence of just how wet I am for her.

"Your scent has been driving me absolutely fucking wild, princess. I wonder if you taste as delicious as you smell."

I'm fairly certain my brain completely short-circuits when she brings her messy fingers to her mouth and sucks my arousal from her. She moans as if it's the best thing to have ever touched her tongue and the sound sets my entire being ablaze. I don't think there's ever been or ever will be, a more seductive creature than the one currently on her knees before me.

"You taste delicious, my precious girl." Her free hand reaches around me and roughly grabs my ass, causing me to let out a startled breath.

Using her hand on my backside, she angles my hips closer towards her. Her fingers tickle their way across my hip and thigh. When she reaches my knee, she hooks her hand behind it and brings it up and over her shoulder. A red blush stains my cheeks, heat warming my pale skin. I'm spread open, right in her face. I try to adjust so that my privates aren't shoved so closely to her but when I do she pulls the fabric tighter against my throat, cutting off my air again.

"This is my pussy now," she looks up at me, desire swirling like serpents around her irises, "and I intend to feast on it whenever I like."

With that, she dives in. Her tongue licks me from back to front in long, languid strokes. She flattens her tongue as she licks towards the back, but then somehow curves it to use just the tip at the end to flick my clit. Again, and again, and again her eager strokes devour every inch of me, driving me towards insanity. My eyes roll back in my head as she pushes inside me. Her slick and firm tongue massages against my inner walls in a way that's completely maddening. She alternates licking and sucking and fucking me with her mouth. I roll my hips against her, desperate for more. My tits ache for attention and I so badly want to bring my hands around to touch them myself but I'm tied up too tightly.

"That's it baby girl," she speaks to me between licks. "Ride my fucking face. Show me what a desperate little whore you are for me."

The ruined cape etches tighter into my skin, my lungs burning and aching with each strangled gasp for air. But every time I feel the sheer panic of needing oxygen, her tongue licks up more of my juices and all my body registers is the pleasure she's driving me towards. Stars dance around the edge of my vision and I can feel a lightness start to settle all the way into my bones. It's like I'm floating outside of my own body.

"Fuck, princess," Morgan's voice sounds far away now, like I'm hearing her through water. "You're such a good slut for me. Your pussy is so wet that it's dripping off my chin and soaking my suit."

Black smoke clouds my vision, the room spins out of focus, and right as I'm about to pass out, she lets go.

The restraint around my neck loosens, allowing air to flood into my lungs. White sparks shoot across my closed eyelids. And then Morgan shoves two fingers roughly inside me. She fucks me fast and hard. The combination of being asphyxiated with the punishing pace of her fingers sends me over the edge. I scream out loud and violently as my entire body spasms with uncontrollable pleasure. It's like I'm floating and falling simultaneously. I dive into an unending sea as wave after wave of pleasure crash through my entire being. My whole pussy pulses over and over again in a seemingly unending climax. And through it all, Morgan never stops her assault, determined to drain every ounce of pleasure from my soul.

My heart rate slows, each breath coming out calmer than the last as I start to come back to reality. My head tilts forward and my eyes meet hers as she looks up at me from between my legs. The sight of this beautiful goddess with her golden hair, beautiful blue eyes, and her perfect, curvy body on her knees for me is almost as good as the orgasm I just had.I don't know what I've done to deserve the attention of a girl like her, but even if it was just for today, what just happened between us was the most amazing thing I've ever experienced.

Fuck. If this is what a climax is supposed to feel like, then what the hell has Kyle been doing to me all these years?

"Are you alright princess?" She cocks her head at me in question, assessing me as if to make sure I'm not broken while carefully pulling herself out of me.

"No," I answer truthfully. "I'm better than alright. That was amazing. I've never had anyone do anything like that to me."

A smile spreads across her stunning face and I'm again struck with how beautiful she is. How did I get lucky enough to ensnare her attention?

She gently places my leg down on the ground and rises to stand in front of me. Pushing hair out of my face and tucking a loose strand behind my ear, she leans down to place a soft kiss against my lips. She tastes like a mix of her and me. I can't help the flutter in my stomach at how filthy and fabulous that knowledge is. Carefully, she removes the red fabric from my neck and unties my hands.

I start to sink to my knees but she pulls me back up, brows furrowing together as she asks, "What are you doing babe?"

"Well, don't I—" I stumble on the words, not really sure how this is supposed to work with another girl. "Shouldn't I do it back to you now?"

She lets out a breathy chuckle before sinking to the ground and picking up my costume. She pulls the fabric up over my body, righting it to make sure I'm as covered as I can be before placing a kiss on my cheek.

"You did so good for me princess. You were such a good girl. But that was a lot for your body. You need to rest and get something to eat and drink before we go for round two."

Insecurities swirl through me, my stomach knotting uncomfortably. I'd messed this up somehow. I was too stupid, too boring and bland. Tears prick my eyes as all the things Kyle has ever criticized me about swarm my mind. I was so stupid, so very foolish to think a girl like her could want someone like me.

"Hey. Hey," her fingers grip my chin, tilting my face up to hers. "Where'd you go?"

"What if… " I swipe a rogue tear away before it can fall. "What if I want to taste you, to please you?"

Something flashes in her eyes, a demon peeking out from beneath the surface. But just as quickly as it is there, it's gone. The haunted house and the draining nature of what we just did must be getting to me.

"Trust me, princess," she steps into me, entering my space and crowding me. Our breasts touch and a new bolt of desire runs through me. "I want that more than you know. I'd kill to have your beautiful face stuck between my thick thighs all night. But first I need to take care of my girl. Why don't we go back to my hotel, get some room service, have a warm bath together, and then I can teach you how to eat cunt like a good little slut?"

I immediately pull back, needing space to breathe.

Needing a moment to think. That sounds amazing, more than amazing actually. That sounds like a damn dream.

Maybe she actually did strangle me and I died and now I'm in Heaven.

But there is a man at home waiting for me. As much as I'd love to leave Kyle behind, run off with Morgan, and never look back, I know that isn't the right thing to do. I spent years with him, and even though I have no intention of staying with him long term, I owe him an explanation. It is the right thing to do.

How can I explain to Morgan that I'm still technically in a relationship and need to break it off, without sending her running from me?

"I'm staying with a friend," I manage to choke out, my eyes trained on the floor beneath my feet. "She'll worry if I don't come back."

"So call her and tell her you won't be back tonight, I'm sure she'll understand." Her hand rubs comforting circles on my back and I can barely stand the touch. I don't deserve her kindness, not while I'm still technically with Kyle.

"Uhm, my phone died and my charger's at her place," my voice comes out as a shaky whisper. My throat feels tight and uncomfortable from what we just did. "Plus, I don't have spare clothes. I can't really walk around in a ruined Red Riding Hood costume, right?"

"Alright," she sounds uncertain. "Can I drive you there then?"

"No," I blurt out quickly, too quickly. "I don't want to leave my car here. Teenagers will vandalize it."

Smooth cover, Scarlett.

I can tell she's not buying it. But she can't really argue with any part of my story. "Okay. Well at least let me walk you to your car," she pulls me into her, wrapping me in a tender embrace. It takes everything in me not to cry. "And if you need me, I'm in room 1202 at The Chrysalis. I'm here for you. Okay?"

I have to fix this. I need to make it right. I can't lose her.

CHAPTER ELEVEN

Scarlett

That was incredible.

My pussy is still throbbing in the best possible way. Everything about Morgan is intoxicating. Being with her feels like driving at top speed with the windows down, it's terrifying and exhilarating all at the same time, and I love it. I've never felt wanted before, not like this.She makes me feel special, like I'm a prize. My heart warms at the thought of us—her and I together. I'ver never thought of myself as gay, but after tonight, there's not a doubt in my mind, I'm meant to be *hers*.

My stomach rolls with unease as I ascend the stairs to my second floor apartment door. I stopped by Sam's to change quickly but then came straight here. I have to get this over with. A light drizzle falls, cooling my heated skin as I take the last few steps. Each footfall is a heavy beat towards a fate I don't want to face. I hate confrontation. I don't want to be with Kyle but my heart definitely belongs to someone else. I've been with him for years, I owe him an explanation. I can't just ghost him, *right*? Part of me wonders if he'll even care. It's always felt like I'm holding him back. Like if he didn't have me tagging along, he'd be free to be who he was meant to be. Maybe he'll be happy that I'm leaving. He can fuck who he wants, whenever he wants. He won't be stuck with me anymore. Maybe this won't be a confrontation at all.

The faded, yellowing door of our apartment is illuminated by a single ancient porch light. The three in the number thirteen on our door hangs slightly askew. Sliding my key into the lock it spins without resistance, telling me it's not locked. He's home. *Fuck.*

Slowly letting the door swing open, I step across the threshold onto the faded carpet. The whole apartment smells of plastic, the only evidence that there have in fact been workers in here fixing our window.

Swirling pain and anxiety hits my heart as I press the door shut. I'm usually greeted by an orange fur ball yelling at me and rubbing up against my legs. He's noticeably absent.

"Samson!" My voice echoes off the wall. There's no response.

Stepping further into the apartment I can see the light

of the TV flashing but the sound is off.

"Samson? Here kitty, kitty, kitty!" I call again, hoping he's just being skittish from all the commotion.

"You're fucking cat isn't here," a deep voice snarls from behind me, making me jump.

I spin to see Kyle standing with one foot crossed over the other in the doorway of the bedroom, his shoulder leaned against the door frame and a bottle in his hand. His usually neatly styled hair is a mess. The dirty blonde locks fall across his forehead. His eyes are red and heavily lidded. He's drunk.

Fuck.

"Where is he?" I take a tentative step back. I know not to challenge him or mess with him when he's acting this way. This isn't the Kyle I fell in love with. When he's been drinking and we're alone, he's different. He's mean.

He pushes off the doorframe, stalking towards me as if I'm the sole reason for all his pain and anger. He's wearing distressed denim and a tight fitting T-shirt. The collar of his shirt is uneven, as if it's been pulled and stretched. He looks off. Not his usual put together self. His rage radiates off him in heated waves. My heart thunders and I'm struck by the urge to run. But I've run before. He always catches me. And when he does, it's always worse.

"Fuck if I know. Stupid thing probably ran out the window and got hit by a car. He's road kill by now."

"Don't say that," I hiss at Kyle as he stalks closer. For every step I take backward he matches with one forward. He's backing me into a corner and there's nothing I can do about it.

"He's as dead as you're going to be if you don't tell me where you were tonight."

Something in me snaps. I'm not sure if it's the sense of power still humming through my blood from my night with Morgan, the promise of a better future, or the fact that he just said my cat is probably fucking dead, but I am done. I'm done with his shit.

I reach out my hands and shove into his chest. He doesn't expect it and stumbles back, hitting the wall behind him.

"Fuck you, Kyle!" I shout, storming past him and into our bedroom. "I'm packing my stuff and I'm leaving. Call me if my cat comes back!"

I remember being so excited when we first moved in here. I had butterflies in my stomach thinking about coming home every night to share my bed with the man who I thought loved me. Now I look around and all I see is a cage—a cage that I allowed myself to stay trapped inside of for far too long. I was too compliant and too silent for too long. But I'm not that girl anymore. I'm ready to stand up for myself and be happy.

Grabbing a duffle bag, I throw it on the bed and begin filling it with all my clothes and shoes. In my peripheral, I can see his dark presence looming in the doorway. I don't turn. I'm done bending to his will.

"Where were you tonight, Scarlett?" His words are slurred and soured. He's angry and drunk. I need to get my shit and get out of here, away from him and all the toxic venom oozing out of every pore of the man I thought I could trust.

I ignore him, continuing to fill the bag with as much as it will hold. I don't even bother to fold anything. I just want to get out of here and to put the past behind me.

A sudden, sharp sting burns my scalp as his fingers thread tightly into my hair. He pulls me back, the motion giving me whiplash. His front is to my back as he holds me securely by the hair, staring down at me with murderous rage in his eyes.

"Where the *fuck* were you tonight, Scarlett?" His other hand snakes down my body and finds the button of the jeans I changed into before coming home. Popping it open, his thick fingers roughly shove their way down the front of my pants. I try to pull away, try to flail, try to fight him—but he's bigger. Tears burn my eyes as my scalp screams from where he holds me tightly by the hair. His calloused fingers find the lips of my pussy. Bile rises in my throat at his unwelcome touch. "Were you off being a whore? Letting someone else touch you?"

"Yes," I spit into his face as I speak with all the pent

up rage I've been holding onto for years. "I was with someone else tonight, Kyle. I'm done with you and this toxic relationship. Now let me go! I'm leaving."

With a firm grip still on my hair he spins me, shoving me face first into the wall. The impact shakes my entire skull, leaving black spots dancing across my field of vision. Everything's fuzzy and off. *Fuck.*

"You're not going anywhere." His fingers find my tender opening and shove their way inside me. I'm dry and closed off but he doesn't care. He finger fucks me roughly and fiercely, desperately trying to draw pleasure from me that isn't there. This is so different from earlier. With Morgan, everything we did was exciting and welcomed. It's like she was unlocking secret pleasures I didn't know I even had. But this feels like a violation, like something is being stolen from me. A choked sob escapes my lips as I try unsuccessfully to throw him off. I don't want him.

"Please. Stop," I sob as he continues his assault.

He rips himself from me, flipping me around and shoving me back against the wall again. Warm wetness pools behind me. *Fuck, I think I'm bleeding.* Inky blackness creeps across my vision, my head throbs in pain as I blink to try to clear my eyes. He's a blurred, black figure looming above me, anger burning off him in a fiery blaze. He's a true monster. Before I can recover, the sharp and sudden sting of a hard slap sends my entire body sideways. I fall to the floor under the force of the backhanded smack to my face.

"You don't get to tell me no, Scarlett." Bending at the waist, he hovers over me. An angry scowl painted across his face, distorting his handsome features into something evil. "You're mine."

"You cheat on me all the time." Everything hurts. Every breath is agony. But I'm not giving in to him. I'm ready to stand up for myself, no matter the cost. "Why do you even care?"

His fingers roughly grip my cheeks, forcing my mouth open into a pained 'O'. He uses his grip to pull me up into him, our lips barely separated. I can taste the stale beer on his breath as he breathes into me.

"You're right. I have cheated on you. And I will continue to cheat on you. And you will take it and then be here waiting to serve me on your fucking knees when I get home," he shoves his tongue into my open mouth, grinding his hardening cock against my leg. "You're an uneducated, weak, mousy little whore, who's worth nothing," he whispers against my lips.

Using all the strength I have left, I rear back away from him and bring my face forward. My forehead collides with cartilage and bone. The unmistakable crunch of his nose against my skin is sickening. Warmth sprays all across me, showering me in red. He screams and releases me to grab his nose.

Seizing the opportunity, I push myself up to my feet.

As quickly as I'm able to, I move towards the front door. I stumble and fall against the walls of the hallway as the entire world spins and twirls. My head throbs and bile rises in my throat. I'm definitely hurt but I have to get out of here. For the first time in a long time I see the future of a life worth living and I'm not willing to give that up easily. I'm going to leave Kyle; leave this apartment. Maybe I'll finally go back to school. I can get a degree, start a career, travel, and see where things go with Morgan. I need to get out of here and give myself the opportunity to finally be free.

And then it all comes crashing down. The weight of his body collides into me, throwing me down to the floor. I hit the ground with a sickening amount of force. The wind is knocked completely from me. My lungs are on fire and vomit burns my esophagus, threatening to escape my mouth. I want to scream and claw away from him, but he's too big, too strong. He throws punch after punch into my head as he pins my body to the ground with his knees. Each hit feels like I'm moving further and further down an endless tunnel, away from the light and freedom at the end. It doesn't even hurt anymore as I teeter on the edge of consciousness.

Wrapping his hand around my hair, he pulls on it. My scalp burns as he attempts to yank me to my feet.

"You're not going anywhere, whore."

I stumble as the entire world seems to tilt and shift beneath my feet. My vision is going in and out. I crawl on all fours, desperately trying to keep up as he pulls me back across the apartment. Blood drips down my face, seeping into my eyes and clouding my sight. The carpet burns my skin as I'm dragged across the bedroom floor.

"Please don't rape me," I manage to mumble between choked sobs.

With a final sharp pull and rough shove, I'm thrown to the floor of the closet. My whole head throbs as the ghost of his touch scorches his violence across my skin. Everything thrums in a viscous rhythm to the beat of my erratic heart.

"I'm not going to rape you. You're a fucking mess. You'll stay in here until you come to your senses and are ready to clean yourself up and service me like I deserve."

The door slams shut, sealing the entire space in cold emptiness. I don't know how long I lay there, bloodied and beaten, until the darkness finally pulls me under.

CHAPTER TWELVE

Morgan

Sleep isn't necessary for a Hell demon, however, I find that my human exterior is more attractive when I let my body rest. My eyes close, my breathing and heart rate lower, and the physical body I have rests. But my mind never shuts off. This means I have a lot of time to think and plot while my body rests. What I should be plotting is how to suck Kyle's soul out through his cock, but my mind can't seem to focus on anything except *her*. I need my thirteenth victim in the next two days. I should be desperately fucking any man I can find, and yet the only person I want is Scarlett.

Last night was my favorite night in all the centuries I've been alive. Sure, I've had nights of depraved pleasure but watching her come all over my face and fingers while I took the air from her lungs, literally, was exhilarating. I've never been so seduced by a single creature before. If I didn't know any better, I'd think she was a temptress sent to steal my soul. I was supposed to spend the evening stealing her. The need to possess her—own her—is overwhelming. But somehow in the process, she claimed me as well. I'd willingly sell my soul to the Devil to have her be mine forever, that is, if the Devil didn't already own my soul.

I have no idea how I'm going to keep her though. How do I explain to her the need to move from town to town, never staying in one place too long? A trail of dead men constantly left in our wake. What woman would sign up to follow a succubus around while she fucks men in order to steal their souls?

A sudden knock at my door slams through my sleeping ears and bangs at the window of my conscious mind.

The "Do Not Disturb" sign is up. They can fuck right off.

My mind wanders back to Scarlett. To her pale skin and ruby red lips. *Fuck*. Those lips are so plump and full. I want to feel those lips wrapped around my clit, suckling and licking and—

The knocking begins again, violently ripping me from my beautiful fantasy. Whoever this is might get their hands torn from their body. With a groan, I open my eyes and roll from the bed. The orange tabby who had been sleeping on top of me scampers off as I angrily throw off the covers. My feet hit the cushioned carpet as I pad across the room. Slipping a large oversized tee over me, I groan as the incessant knocking continues.

"Coming!" I growl at the closed door.

I rip the door open so swiftly, it bangs on the wall behind. Ready to scream at the motherfucker who interrupted my tantalizing fantasy, I'm stopped by the face looking back at me from the other side of the doorway.

She's beautiful. She'll always be beautiful to me, no matter what, but the purple bruises blooming across her face are ugly. They paint a picture of violence across her pale cheeks. I see red as I look at her. Nothing this sweet and innocent should look so... *broken*.

"What the hell happened?" I seethe as I usher Scarlett into my room.

"I'm sorry to bother you. I just didn't know where else to go and you told me your hotel room number and I just came here without thinking." She's nervously ranting, pacing in small circles, and wringing her delicate little fingers. However, I stopped listening the moment she said she was scared and ran to me. I'm a fucking Hell demon, not a god damned angel, but fuck if it doesn't feel good to be her savior. I desperately want to be her safe place, her home, her heart. I want to be hers.

"Princess," I cross the room and press my palm lightly against her shoulder to stop her pacing. "I'm glad you came here. Let's sit down, okay?"

Draping my arm around her, I usher her toward the bed. Together we sit on the edge as I wrap my fingers around her shoulder and let her weight ease into me. I loved seeing her needy and writhing in agonizing pleasure last night, but this feeling of her right here leaning on me, makes me feel *really* good, like I'm needed for more than just a good fuck. I curl my arm around her tightly and she lets out a sweet little sigh. I could hold her for the rest of eternity and never get sick of her comforting warmth for a single moment.

Without warning, a flash of orange flies into her lap. She jumps, startled by the flying ball of fur that just launched itself at her. I try to shoo the cat away but he hisses at me and begins using his paws to knead at my girl's lap.

"Oh my god! Samson?" Scarlett looks to be somewhere on a spectrum of emotions that ping-pongs between shock and relief. "This is my cat!" Her eyes fly to my face. "Why the fuck do you have my cat?"

"This is your cat? I found him wandering the street and he looked so hungry I took him in." *Smooth cover.* I can't exactly tell her that I broke the window of her apartment to stop her shithead boyfriend from raping her and then her cat insisted on coming home with me.

That'd be weird to admit, right?

"I thought I'd lost him. There was an accident at my apartment, the window was blown out. When I went back last night he was gone and I assumed he'd gotten out the broken window and was missing." A tear rolls down her face. She snuggles into Samon's orange fur, holding him tightly. He purrs happily in her arms. "Thank you so much for saving him. I'd be lost without him."

My heart aches watching her be so vulnerable. I want to break the bones of every creature that's ever harmed her.

"What happened Scarlett? When you went home last night, how did you get hurt?"

Her scent is strange. It's still her, the rich and addictive smell of coffee and caramel, but there's something else, something that wasn't there last night. I can't put my finger on it, but it smells *feminine* somehow. It's not her sweet magnolia scent of fear. This is new. I want to turn her face to mine, to look into her eyes and see what has changed in her, but I sense she might need something different. I let her stare off into nothingness, losing herself somewhere in her mind for a moment. I simply sit and hold her, letting her have the time and space she needs to process.

"There was a guy." I know this but I don't tell her that. I just sit and rub small circles on her back while she talks. Samson has curled up in her lap and she absentmindedly strokes his fur while she talks. "We dated for a while. We lived together. That's why I ran last night. It'd been over for a while, I'm now realizing, but I needed to say it out loud. I needed him to hear it."

I nod. Letting her continue without judgment or

interruption.

"He was drunk when I got home. I know he's cheated on me. I've never caught him in the act, but it's obvious, you know? So I didn't really think he'd care that I was leaving, but he freaked out."

I can feel my barbs prick against my inner walls in anticipation. The monster and me agree—we're going to fuck Kyle up and suck his soul. Then we're going to fuck his girl and steal her away, riding off into a bloody, smutty sunset.

"Freaked out, how sweetheart?" I don't want to push her, but I need to hear her say it. We need to work through it, together.

"He hit me," her voice is so small it pains me to hear. A single tear rolls down her cheek. "I told him I met someone and I was leaving. I'm so stupid. I expected him to be relieved to see me go. But he was so angry. He told me that if he couldn't have me, no one would. He hit me and I fell down. He dragged me by the hair to the bedroom and locked me in the closet. I sat there all night in the dark, terrified he'd come back. But then I heard him leave for work. I used one of my necklaces to unscrew the door handle and I just ran. I didn't even get to grab my things."

She breaks down sobbing and when she can't continue speaking I just hold her, letting her cry into my shoulder. I have nothing to say that would comfort her in this moment. All I can think to do is just hold her.

"I'll take care of him, princess. I promise you." I'm unsure if she just doesn't hear me, or doesn't register the words of my threat but she doesn't respond. We sit in silence, holding each other, for what feels like an eternity.

I should spend the day claiming my thirteenth victim. I now know where Kyle is, it would be so easy to 'accidentally bump into him,' and convince him to take me home. He just lost his girlfriend to someone else, he's probably vulnerable and looking for an anger-fuck. But when I look down at the delicate little creature in my arms I know I can't leave her right now. This girl holds what's left of my Hellish heart in her hands, and today she needs me.

I spent the entire day pampering my princess. We went down to the salon and got pedicures, then we ordered room service and binged terrible reality shows. Sitting in a plush hotel robe in bed, snacking on french fries, while watching my girl giggle uncontrollably at some stupid show, was the lightest I'd felt in as long as I could remember. It was a nearly perfect afternoon.

Things with her are just easy. There are no awkward pauses or uncomfortable moments, it is as if our souls have been seeking each other's company and now have finally found where they were meant to be. Which is ridiculous because I don't even have a soul. I have a Hell beast who eats men's souls through their cocks instead, but a girl can dream, right?

Scarlett showered and is now doing her hair and make up while I patiently wait for her in the main room. The cat is allowed in there with her but I was shooed out in the name of 'privacy.' Eventually she'll have to get over the need for privacy. If she's naked somewhere, then that's where I intend to be. But for today, I'll let her get ready alone.

She enters the room looking fucking gorgeous. My mouth drops open slightly as I take her in. She's in a tight black dress that hugs her slight curves and petite little waist perfectly. The green hues she chose for her smoky-eye look make her warm brown eyes pop and she chose that damn red lipstick, again. I want to fling her onto the bed and lick her sweet little cunt dry but I promised her a nice dinner date.

Her scent is still strange. Something is definitely different about her tonight but I can't figure out what it could be.

"Sit," I command, turning my back to her so I don't lose my will and start playing with my pretty girl and her perfect perky tits before we even make it out the door. "I'll make you a drink."

Making us two whiskey gingers, I let my mind wander and envision how everyone will be staring at the beautiful girl I get to proudly display on my arm. My princess and I will certainly turn heads. But she's mine, and only mine.

That knowledge has me giddy. I make her drink a double. I don't want her drunk necessarily, but I'd love for her to be tipsy, her inhibitions lowered, ready to let me play with her however I want tonight. Maybe I'll tie her to the bed and bring out the toys. She liked breath play, I wonder how she'd feel about being a good little girl and laying across my lap while I spank her?

As I spin back around with our drinks, Scarlett winces, holding her lower stomach. Her eyes close and wrinkles crease her forehead in a clear expression of pain as her hand cradles her lower abdomen. My mind spirals with intrusive anxiety inducing thoughts. Did he hit her more than just on her face? Or worse, violate her? Fuck, if he fucking hurt that precious fucking pussy, *MY* precious fucking pussy, I'll kill him. I mean, I'm going to kill him either way but if he touched what's mine I will gut him like a damn pig, crack his ribcage open, and feast on his fucking organs while he watches. His last vision on this earth will be me taking bloody bites out of his spleen.

I quickly put our drinks down and rush to her. I kneel in front of her and rest my palms on her warm thighs. "What's wrong princess? Are you hurt? Did he hurt you more?" My words come out in a jumbled rush but I can't help it. She makes me feel out of control.

She let's a shy little laugh. "It's not that babe."

Confusion wraps around me, constricting my chest. I

need to protect her and make sure she's okay. I'd do anything, kill anyone, fight any monstrous threat, to keep my girl safe and happy. That thought is almost as terrifying as thinking about her being hurt.

I haven't felt this strongly about someone in centuries. The last time I felt this level of obsession it ended in pain, heartbreak, and something so sinister it almost broke me entirely. Last time I was in love, I was betrayed. I was so blind with rage at his betrayal that I sold my soul to the Devil in exchange for revenge. So yeah, I'm terrified. But she's worth the risk.

"What is it then, princess? What do you need?"

A slight blush stains her pale cheeks and the sight is absolutely, sinfully delicious. She's so sweet and innocent. The monster in me roars to life at the thought of her tied up, helpless, dripping with desire, and covered in red marks. Corrupting this sweet little princess will be my favorite indulgence for as long as she'll let me.

"Um," she's nervous, looking anywhere but at me. "It's just cramps."

"Cramps?" I'm confused. Muscle cramping? From what?

"Yeah," her blush intensifies, red rippling down the slender column of her throat. I want to lick her neck and see if the reddened skin is warm under my tongue. "Like period cramps. I, um, got my period this morning and the cramps are brutal, even though I already took some Ibuprofen."

She winces again as her uterus clenches and unclenches inside her. The knowledge unleashes something completely unhinged inside of me. All the air leaves my lungs as if I'm drowning in a sea of lust. My heart pounds aggressively in my ears, thrumming with need. My mouth is dry but my cunt is fucking soaked. Before I can even register what I'm doing, I have her trapped beneath me. One of my hands holds both her wrists above her head while my thighs balance on either side of her thin form, pinning her to the bed beneath me.

"You're bleeding?" My voice is more of a growl than anything, the monster inside pushing its way to the surface. I blink rapidly, willing my eyes to stay a stormy blue and not shift to a demonic red.

"Well, I mean yeah, like a normal period amount." Her eyes scan my face, trying to figure out why the mood has shifted.

The increase of her heart rate, the seductive puffs of her nervous little breaths, the knowledge that her scent changed, which I picked up on earlier, is because her pretty little pussy is slick and red is driving me to the point of complete lustful madness. I mean I'm a damn succubus with a Hell demon living inside me, taking the place of my soul. Blood lust is pretty normal. However, this level of an absolutely consuming need for someone whose soul I can't even suck is…*new*. But I have no intention of trying to hold back when it comes to her.

My mouth falls to her neck, my teeth sinking into her tender flesh. I bite and suck while running my tongue over her pulse point, letting the erratic pace thunder against my tongue. She shrieks but her cries quickly turn to moans as her pain morphs into pleasure. With her focus on the sensations my mouth is giving her, I let my fingers slide swiftly into her panties. I rub my fingers through her folds.

"Fuck princess," I moan against her ear as I push a single finger inside her tight pussy. "You're so slick."

"Did you not hear me?" She pants between moans of pleasure. "I'm on my period. I'll get you gross."

Gross? How could this beautiful angel ever think I'd call her gross? Her lack of self awareness fucking angers me beyond belief.

She screams as I shift my weight to be right on top of her, dominating her. I get in her face, my forehead pressed to hers and our eyes locked onto each other's. I lean more weight onto her wrists, holding her down tightly. I know it probably hurts a little, but I don't give a fuck. I finger fuck her slick, tight pussy roughly as I stare possessively into her soul.

"I told you, this is my pussy." I shove a second finger inside her, fucking her fast and hard. Her back arches off the bed and she moans loudly. "I will fuck it whenever I want." I curl my fingers against her plump mound of nerves, massaging that spot inside that makes her pretty little painted toes curl. "And the fact that it's red and ready for me just makes me want you that much more."

I crash my lips against hers in a desperate kiss. Pushing my tongue against her mouth, I demand access to yet another one of her holes. My good girl opens for me, letting me sweep my tongue into her needy little mouth. The kiss is possessive, claiming, animalistic. She's mine now and I have no intention of ever letting this beautiful creature escape me. I grind my tongue against hers, pulsing in time with the pace of my fingers in her pussy. Pretty soon we're a writhing mess of tongues and fingers, our hips grinding against each other.

"Please," she begs me in her sweet, breathy voice. "Please babe, can you do that thing you did last night?"

I smirk down at the sweet little princess beneath me, begging a demon to eat her cunt.

"You mean when I licked your pretty pussy, princess?"

"Yes," Scarlett moans, as I ram my fingers roughly into her again and again. "Please, that felt so good. I want that again."

"Did Kyle," *his* name drips off my tongue like poison, "not do a good job taking care of your cunt?" I ask as I lick a long and slow path up her neck to her ear.

"No—" she screams as I bite and suck at her neck. That'll definitely leave yet another mark. *Good.* "He, uh never, I mean, no one has ever," she stumbles over her words as a flush crawls across her skin.

"What are you embarrassed of, little one?" I still my fingers inside her, refusing to continue until she answers me. She huffs in frustration before relenting.

"I've only ever *been* with Kyle, no one else. And with him it was just only ever, you know, regular old sex. Like me on my back and him on top. I'm not sure I've ever even come during sex until last night." Her cheeks flush a violently beautiful shade of crimson.

"Am I the first to get to taste your pussy?"

Mine. Mine. Mine.

"Yes. And if it's okay, I'd like for you to taste it again?"

She doesn't need to ask me twice.

Removing my fingers from inside her slickness, I bring them up and hold them above my face. Scarlett is still pinned tightly beneath me, I want her to watch, to see first hand how deeply I want to taste her right now. Keeping my eyes locked on hers, I bring my bloodied fingers to my face. The smell is fucking maddening. It's still her sweet caramel scent with a hint of bitter coffee mixed in, but now it's mixed with a strong feminine scent. *Fuck me*, that smell is the most enticing thing to ever enter my gustatory system.

Her expression shifts from horrified to turned on as I put her bloodied fingers to my mouth and let my tongue skim the potent mix of her blood and arousal from my fingers. My pussy pulses in intense need as soon as her taste lands on my tongue. She's the sweetest fucking thing I've ever had in my mouth. I can't help my eyes closing, my head falling back, and a satisfied moan leaving my lips as lick and suck every last drop of her from me. The monstrous Hell beast inside is panting desperately and yet my barbs feel safely tucked away. It's as if he too wants to taste her, but not consume her.

His growl reverberates across my mind. *"More. More. Mine. She's mine."*

She is fucking mine. All fucking mine. A smile pulls at the corner of my lips and the fingers pop from my mouth as I realize that there's nothing now to stop me from claiming her. Kyle is gone. She chose me. She *wants* me.

I quickly jump off her, my eyes scanning up and down her lithe form.

"Too many clothes," I snap at her before ripping her tight little strapless dress down her body. She gasps as I pull the fabric down her thin form, exposing her cute little tits. They're so pink and perky and still covered in my bite marks.

"Here's what's going to happen, princess," when I reach her period panties, I hook my fingers in the waistband and pull them off with her dress. "I'm going to crawl between those pale, pretty thighs and feast on your bleeding pussy until you come all over my face. And then you're going to get on your knees and please me, do you understand?"

She nods her head enthusiastically. Her tongue peaks out to lick her lips. The scent of her arousal is so strong I can taste it on my tongue.

"Words, princess. I need your words." I drop to my

knees, hooking my hands behind her bent legs and pulling her to the edge of the bed.

"Yes, please. Please Morgan, I need you."

She *needs* me. She has no idea what those words do to me. To be needed. Not just wanted for a quick fuck, but to be truly needed by another, that's something I'm not sure I've ever had.

I let my hand skim the length of pale flesh on her thigh slowly, teasingly. Goosebumps erupt across her skin and she lets out the cutest little whine. My fingers gently caress the lips of her pussy in long, light strokes. I can feel her pussy weeping for me already.

"So desperate for me to make you come. Such a fucking slut for my tongue, aren't you princess?

"Yes. Please."

I let my fingers pull her lips wide apart, exposing all of her to me. She's dripping wet and a light sheen of red is spread all over her pretty pussy.

"Say it," I command her. "Say you're my whore."

"Please, Morgan. I'll be your good little whore. Just please make me come."

I dive into her without any pretense, licking and sucking as I kiss her pussy up and down. She writhes and moans as my mouth assaults her in a flurry of lips, teeth, and tongue. Her taste is even better when freshly licked from her bloody cunt. It's sweet and rich and the more I have in my mouth, the more I want. When my tongue circles her hole she arches with need. I let it slide away, up to her clit, flicking it back and forth rapidly. She screams and her hands fly to her tits, rubbing and pulling her hardened nipples. She's so needy for me everywhere.

If only I could tongue-fuck her and lick her clit at the same time.

A devious idea crosses my mind. Her eyes are closed and her head is thrown back in ecstasy. Even when my teeth nibble lightly on her clit, she keeps her eyes closed, concentrating on not coming too soon. She wouldn't even notice if I partially shifted. My demon hums in agreement, desperate to taste her too. I continue to lick and suck her pussy while focusing on shifting only my tongue, nothing more. We don't need the full demon coming out to play.

Removing my tongue from her briefly so she won't feel the shift, I feel it lengthen in my mouth. The tip splits as it shifts into the monstrous forked tongue of my inner beast. Then I dive back in. One end circles her pulsating, bloodied hole, while the other flicks and strokes her needy little buddy. She gushes with wetness for me as I drive her to the edge of insanity.

"Oh my god! Oh my god!" she chants as I use my thick demon tongue to bring her close to the edge.

"There's no god here baby. Now come all over my face and let me lick it all up."

If only you knew what kind of monster you have between your legs, my sweet girl.

I shove my tongue inside her, letting both ends move freely. She instantly falls over the edge. Her climax causes her entire body to stiffen. She screams my name and the sound is my new favorite song. I might be a succubus but she's a damn siren with the way she sings out my name as she falls into a sea of ecstasy. I stroke both sides of her walls, coaxing every last wave of pleasure I can from her. Her cum and blood coat my entire mouth in a delicate feast.

When she finally comes down, I remove my tongue from inside her. I will the demon back inside, letting my two tips fuse back into one, normal, human tongue. My girl is a panting mess on the bed. When our eyes meet I can see the fear and lust swirling in her vision. I must look like a monster with her cum and blood covering my face but she seems to like it.

Standing to my full height, I rip my top off over my head, exposing my full breasts and hardened nipples. Her eyes fall to my tits and she squirms, clearly wanting a taste of me.

"My turn, princess. Come over here and get on your knees like my good little slut."

CHAPTER THIRTEEN

Scarlett

Morgan's the most gorgeous woman I've ever seen. She's so powerful and seductive. Her hips sway as she walks to the other side of the room, entrancing me as she moves to perch on the edge of a plush bench. She sits gracefully, staring at me, completely fucking naked. My pussy is still throbbing from the orgasm that just ripped through me, stealing the air from my lungs. I've never felt pleasure like that before. The way she plays with my body, knowing exactly where to touch and stroke me, is like nothing else I've ever experienced. And her heated gaze continues to make it difficult for me to catch my breath.

She spreads her legs wide, showing me her dripping wet pussy. Her pink folds glisten in the soft white light of the hotel room. My mouth goes dry. I'm desperate to please her. Her lips curl into a sinister smirk and her eyes glint with mischief. It's a look that I'm beginning to crave. God, I love that look.

"On your knees," she commands as her perfectly manicured fingers slide over her round tits. "Crawl to me." She caresses her own breasts, her fingers tweaking her nipples as she stares me in the eye, sinful lust swirling around her irises. "Now!"

I'm helpless to obey. Sinking to my knees, I bend at the waist and place my palms on the thick carpet. I'm naked and vulnerable, my tits swinging with each move forward and my ass sticking in the air. And yet, I've never felt sexier. Her heated focus on me burns into my skin, searing every nerve in my body. The normally calm seas of her eyes have shifted into something passionately chaotic. *They're mesmerizing.* This goddess of a woman wants me, craves me. And that knowledge has me feeling more powerful than I've ever felt. I feel confident for the first time in my life.

I stop and kneel between her legs. Holding her gaze, I shift my ass onto the backs of my legs and place my palms on my thighs, waiting for her command.

"You want to be a good girl and make me come?" she asks me as she continues to tweak her own stiffened pink nipples. My eyes fall to her bare pussy, spread wide for me. My mouth suddenly waters. I *need* to taste her.

"Yes. I mean…" Heat rises in my cheeks as I become nervous again, second-guessing what I should do. "I've never done this with another girl before so I don't know how, but I want to try."

She smiles down at me, assessing me. The sweet scent of jasmine which is so unmistakably her, wraps around me and comforts me.

"You're perfection. My perfect little princess on her knees for me," she cocks her head to the side, like a predator sizing up their prey. "Touch me, Scarlett."

Her praise gives me a slight confidence boost and I shuffle closer, splaying my palms on the tops of her thighs. She licks her lips in anticipation, watching with hunger as I stroke across her soft skin. She's so soft. I've never touched a woman this intimately before and the feeling is surprisingly comforting. With Kyle I always felt awkward and like I didn't know how to touch his body. But with Morgan, there's a certain freedom in understanding how another female's body feels.

My goddess nods ever so slightly, giving me permission to taste and touch. My hands caress her curved hips as I bring my mouth down on her breast. Her hand wraps around the back of my head, her fingers sliding into my hair, tugging slightly as I trace my tongue along the curved valley of her flesh. Her nipple hardens further under the attention, the sensation against my tongue making me crave more of her.

"Fuck," she breathes out on an exhale as I let my teeth

lightly skim the stiffened bud. "That's it baby girl, just like that."

I move to her other breast, giving it the same attention, until she's moaning and writhing against me. Her hands hold me tightly against her, my sensitive breasts grazing against her skin every time she rolls her body against mine. I can't help the cry of pleasure that I spill against her curves. I'm driving myself just as crazy as I am her. I just came incredibly hard and yet I feel my aching pussy leaking down my thighs again as we grind against each other.

Pulling me off of her, she looks down at me. "Do not move. I need to get something but you're going to be my good little girl and wait right here for me, aren't you?"

I nod eagerly, licking my lower lip in anticipation for whatever comes next. My beautiful mistress stands, trailing her fingers down my face to my chin. Her fingers lightly brush against my jaw as she tilts my head up until our eyes meet. Leaning down, she kisses me softly. Her lips are just a whisper against mine. The kiss is tender and yet, so possessive. It's like she's claiming me as hers and promising to take care of me at the same time.

"How'd I get so lucky to get such a good girl?" she murmurs against my lips. "I'm never letting you get away, princess. You belong to me."

I nod. She's right. Somehow over the past few days, I've fallen helplessly under her spell.

I sit as still as possible while she rummages around the

room behind me. My clit throbs with need and I have to fight the urge to rub my thighs together to seek relief. But, I want to be her good girl. I want to please her. So I sit still, biting my lower lip, and refusing to move until she comes back.

Suddenly her sharp nails scrape lightly down the length of my spine. I arch my back at her shiver-inducing touch. My small breasts are pushed out with the movement. She takes the opportunity to strike. Two sharp stings land across my chest. The pain radiates out from my tender nipples across each of my breasts. I moan loudly and the stinging pleasure she is able to pull from my body.

"Such a sweet, desperate slut for me, aren't you?"

"Yes!" I pant. I'd give anything, do anything, for her to keep touching me. I absolutely am desperate for her.

"Open your knees wide," she commands. I readily comply.

She bends down behind me, her body wrapping around mine. Her blonde hair falls across my shoulders, a stark contrast to my raven locks. We couldn't be more opposite— lightness and darkness. Yet, we seem to fit together so well. She kisses and nips at my neck. The feel of her tongue and teeth on my delicate pressure point is intoxicating. I'm addicted to this woman, and I don't think I'll ever be free of her spell. I'm absolutely and completely ruined for all others. She's right—*I'm hers.*

Taking my hand in hers, she wraps it around something hard and plastic. "You're going to hold this wand to your pretty little pussy while I ride your face. You're not allowed to remove it until you make me come. Do you understand, princess?"

I don't. I don't know what a wand is. But, I do know I want to please her, so I nod in agreement.

She rises and saunters around me to sit back on the bench in front of me. Tucking a loose strand of hair behind my ear, she stares down at me. Heated desire burns so brightly in her eyes that I'd swear her irises are ringed with red.

Leaning down she reaches between my legs, pushing something on the object she has wedged against my core. Immediately, harsh vibrations pulse against me, causing my entire body to thrum with energy.

"Oh fuck," I moan loudly as the wand hums against my tender folds.

"You're going to hold that right there. Do not move it until I tell you. Do you understand?"

I nod, unable to form coherent words or thoughts as heat coils in my core.

"Now stick out your tongue. I'm going to teach you to eat cunt like a good little slut."

Her filthy words send me spiraling further towards the edge. Everything about her is powerful and radiant. Her golden waves cascade across her shoulders, shimmering as she repositions herself and tilts her hips up towards my face. I follow her instructions, sticking out my tongue. I can barely focus on anything besides the pounding vibrations assaulting me with pleasure but when she slides her fingers into my hair and drags my face towards her glistening pink pussy, my focus turns completely to her. I'd do anything she tells me to do, I'd follow her to Hell and back if it meant I could keep living in this state of euphoric bliss that she elicits.

"Lick me, all the way up my slit, sweet girl."

My tongue hits her softness and her taste immediately explodes in my mouth. She tastes sweet, like vanilla. I hum against her, which I guess she likes, because she sucks in a sharp inhale. I drag my tongue slowly up, lapping up as much of her wetness as I can. She moans loudly and I look up to see her throw her head back in pleasure. The power I feel on my knees for her is unlike anything I've ever experienced before. Whenever I've given a blowjob to Kyle it always felt like I was being used. Like I was only there for him to use. But right now on my knees for her, watching this goddess lose control because of *me*, I feel like a goddamn queen.

"Baby, your tongue is incredible. You feel so fucking good. Don't stop."

I don't. I explore every delicate inch of her soft flesh I can reach with my tongue. I want to pull every last drop of pleasure from her body and drink it down greedily. Her clit swells under my attention and I can't help myself from sucking the throbbing bud between my lips.

"Shit!" she screams, her hips writhing against me. "That's it baby. You're so fucking perfect."

Her praise wraps around me, surrounding me in warmth. I can't help the heat building at the base of my spine. Her taste on my tongue, her moans in my ears, and the vibrations on my pussy are too much. Pleasure is rapidly building inside me.

"I'm going to come," I whisper into her folds.

Her fingers pull at the stands of my hair, stinging my scalp. My head is yanked back so our eyes meet. Her arousal drips from my lips and down my chin. The red in her eyes is more pronounced now. It should scare me, but all I think about is how badly I want to shatter with my tongue shoved deep inside her.

"You can come all you want but do not remove that wand until I've finished and drenched that pretty little face in my cum, do you understand me?"

"Ye—yes," I manage to choke out. My orgasm is building swiftly, I'm not sure I can contain it much longer.

"Let me see you come while you're on your knees for me, princess."

And I do. The world goes dark as my orgasm crashes into me. Wave after wave of intense pleasure shoots through my entire body. I moan and ride the wand between my legs until the last crescendo of ecstasy ebbs away.

"Fuck!" I scream out into the void of darkness surrounding me.

And then she finds me in the darkness, her touch

dragging me back to her—where I belong.

"So beautiful, sweet girl. Do you know just how fucking beautifully you come undone?"

My heavy eyes open and I'm met with the eyes of a lustful demon. Red rings of desire burn the whites of her eyes, their focus solely on me. The heat of her stare is enough to consume me entirely and leave me as nothing but a pile of ash at her feet.

My pussy still throbs with the intensity of the orgasm and I try to move the wand away. Her slender fingers fall to my wrist stopping me. I whine but she doesn't relent. She forces me to hold the wand against myself.

"Not until I've come. Now get back over here and fuck me with that pretty pink tongue."

She leans back on the bench. The position draws my attention to the stiff peaks of her hardened nipples. I can't stop staring at her tits. They're so big and round and absolutely fucking perfect. As I take in the powerful goddess spread before me, desire winds in my lower stomach again. The vibrations become less over stimulating and more welcoming. I've never experienced this before, this wanting of someone even after I've just come for them—*twice.*

Fuck, my desire for her seems to be fucking endless.

"Fold your tongue lengthwise, so the two sides curve up towards each other," she demands, her eyes falling to my mouth. I comply, sticking my tongue out for her assessment.

"Good girl. Now you're going to keep it just like that and put it in me, curl it, and rub my inner walls until I cover your pretty little face in cum, got it?"

I nod. Then dive in. It takes me a moment to figure out how to enter her but as her tight opening squeezes around my tongue, it's like I've gone to Heaven. I drive myself into her, curling and rubbing like she said to do and I can feel her warmth squeeze around me. Her pussy throbs and pulses around my tongue and she moans loudly when I rub a certain spot on her insides with the tip. So I do it again. And again.

"Fuck! Fuck! Princess, keep that up and I'm going to come."

I want to make her come. My own crescendo is rising again and I want her to fall with me this time. I bring my free hand up to her clit. Gathering some of the wetness from where my tongue is fucking her tight little hole, I rub small circles around the hardened bud.

"Shit! That's it baby, don't stop!" she directs from above me.

I don't think I could even if I wanted to. I'm completely mesmerized at the power I hold as I make her come undone. I use my tongue to massage her inner walls and my fingers to rub her clit. She's breathing heavily and writhing violently against me. The way we're fucking eachother is messy and aggressive and almost animalistic. But it feels so fucking good.

With a final, hard grind with my tongue, I feel her pussy grab on to me tightly. Her inner walls spasming violently.

"Fuck!" she screams as she shatters for me.

Her sweet vanilla taste explodes out of her and onto my face as she comes. The knowledge that I'm covered in her release pushes me over the edge with her and I lose myself into the lustful madness once again, this time with my tongue buried in her cunt. My mind goes completely blank as pleasure consumes my entire body, rushing through me like fire in my veins.

I'm drawn back down as her hands wrap around me. She pulls the wand away and I hear it thud against the floor off in the distance. My vision is blurred by the tears stinging my eyes. My whole body is shaking. It was so much, almost too much, and yet I can't wait to do it again. I want to experience anything she's willing to give me.

She pulls me into her lap. "You did so good for me baby," she croons into my ear softly as she strokes my head and back in a soft and soothing rhythm. My heart beats rapidly in my chest, each thump feeling like it belongs entirely to the woman wrapped around me. "*My* good girl."

CHAPTER FOURTEEN

Morgan

"Favorite ice cream flavor?"

Scarlett's giggle is officially one of my new favorite sounds in the entire fucking universe, second only to her screams of pleasure. I've spent a long time in this world and never once have I felt so completely enraptured by a simple conversation with another person. It's like all the light in the room emanates from her smile. I can't seem to pull away from her brightness, it draws me into her orbit too deeply.

Scarlett thinks for a long moment before deciding. "Mint chocolate chip is probably my favorite. Crunching the chips between your back teeth while letting the cool mint melt and tingle on your tongue is fun."

She might like a little sensation play. Keeping that little piece of information for a rainy day.

The thought strikes me like a fucking bullet to the gut—*I'm keeping her.* There's no part of me that thinks this is just until I get my thirteenth victim and leave this town. If I leave, I'm taking her. If Scarlett wants to stay, I will find a way to stay. She is mine and I'm not fucking letting her go.

I've had playthings over the years. Temporary bodies to fill my bed and keep my pussy sated between victims. Some have been beautiful and exotic women, others handsome and strong men. I only suck from pieces of shit, so those who have a pure soul are safe from the demon within me. I've enjoyed each of them. One particularly handsome Spanish male warmed my bed for roughly a decade, off and on, before I finally had to leave Europe and leave him behind. He never once asked how I never aged a day and he never asked for more than a night of passion. He was almost perfect. But never, not in the centuries that I've walked this Earth, has a creature called to me as Scarlett does. It's as though the soul I once had was destined to be hers. And now that I've finally found her, I'm not letting her get away. I want to own every single piece of her—every breath she takes, every pumping ounce of blood in her veins, every hope and wish that crosses her mind, all of her *needs* to be mine. I want to consume every ounce of her until there ceases to be her and me, and there is just *us*.

"What's yours?" she asks, her cute little fingers skating across the bare skin of my arm.

"What?" My thoughts drifted too far away. I lost track of the conversation while staring at her delicate curves barely covered by the loose sheet and thinking of how to keep her.

She giggles again. *Fuck*, that sound does things to me.

"What's your favorite ice cream flavor? I told you mine, now it's your turn." She playfully swats at my arm. The urge to grab her wrists, pin her down, and lick her delicious cunt until she comes on my face again is almost overwhelming. But, I should probably give her a break...for now.

"Strawberry."

"Strawberry?" she asks incredulously. Her eyes go wide and a smirk pulls at the corners of her mouth.

"Yeah. What's wrong with strawberry?"

"There's nothing wrong with it, it's just so...*normal*. It's just, like, boring and sweet and you're so...not." She giggles again.

This sweet seductress with her cute little laugh will be my ruin.

I roll on top of her, pinning her arms above her head, both wrists in one of my hands. The look of shock on her face is intoxicating. If I could keep her tied up between my thighs for the rest of eternity, I would.

"Say strawberry is boring again," I challenge in the deep and commanding tone that I know makes her pretty pussy weep for me.

She cocks an eyebrow at me. Rolling her lips as if

thinking through her options. "Strawberry is a boring as fuck favorite ice cream flavor."

Brat.

I dive in. I use my free hand to poke at her ribs, tickling the shit out of her. She giggles and wheezes, bucking her hips to try to displace me and get free, but I have her trapped. She squirms and squeals as I pepper her with kisses and tickling touches.

"Stop! Stop!" she finally chokes out between laughs. I pull back to look at her and am caught off guard by the depths of her eyes. The browns of her irises are streaked with flecks of warm gold that shimmer in the light. Just like the rest of her—her eyes are a little darkness and a little light.

After a beat she finally smiles at me, illuminating the dark caverns of my Hell stained soul with her warmth. "I like you."

I smile in return. "Good, I'd hope so after you let me lick that sweet little cunt repeatedly." I raise an eyebrow at her.

"No I'm serious," she turns her gaze down and sinks her teeth into her lower lip. I want to rip that plump lip from under her own teeth and bite down on it. I don't like that she's being shy with me. I want her to always be comfortable. I rub my palms softly up and down her arms, comforting her. After our fabulous fucking session, she put her underwear back on but nothing else, and now I can see her nipples start to stiffen beneath the light fabric of the sheet. "I really like you."

"I like you too, princess."

In fact, I'm falling for you.

The words are on the tip of my tongue. I want to tell her that she's snaked her way into the empty pit where my soul once lived and found a part of me that I thought had been lost long ago.

"Can I ask you something kind of personal?" She changes the subject quickly, saving us from a conversation that maybe we're both not ready to have yet.

"Define 'kind of personal' and maybe I'll think about answering."

She rolls her eyes at me, a smile tugging her perfect little pout.

I'm going to have to tame my little brat.

"What's your question, princess?"

She rakes her teeth across her bottom lip clearly considering whether or not she actually wants to ask. She's so fucking cute. "What do you *do*?"

"You mean, besides you?"

"Stop!" She playfully slaps my arm. "I mean, what do you do for work? This hotel, the room service, the closet full of designer clothes. All those things are expensive. I was just curious."

"There are some people willing to pay a lot of money to find out just how faithful their spouse is or isn't. I help them. They pay me well for the information I'm able to provide them."

"So you're like a private investigator?"

"Something like that, princess. I'm compensated well, even if the news I deliver isn't exactly what my clients were hoping for. And there are some people I work for, who pay extra for some extra services."

Like disposing of their unfaithful dickhead husbands.

Sometimes my victims find me, like Kyle. Assholes that the universe seems to throw my way in order to rid the earth of their miserable existence. Other times I'm paid to *take care* of a man, make him disappear for a lover who's been wronged. The paid jobs keep me living very comfortably. And, as long as I keep moving from town to town, place to place, no one ever tracks the mysterious murders back to me.

I expect her to ask questions, to try to pry the lid off of Pandora's Box and bring all my Hellish truths to the surface, but instead a yawn escapes her perfectly rounded lips. Her yawns are cute. They make her forehead crinkle in a way that makes my stomach flutter. Sensing the shift in mood, the giant orange fur ball leaps to her lap. He prances around her upper thighs, tail held high, clearly indicating that I will not, in fact, be getting any more action tonight. He finally settles, curling up into a ball on her stomach and purring loudly. If I wasn't so impressed with his need to protect my precious princess, I'd be more annoyed with him.

"Are you tired?" I ask, pushing a raven lock off her

cheek, and tucking it behind her ear. She has tiny, red, heart gems in her ears. The glimmering red stones match her beautiful ruby lips. "I can turn off the lights, move to the second bed, and we can go to sleep if you want?"

Her hand immediately shoots out to grab mine, her eyes flying open. "Please, stay in bed with me?" There's such vulnerability in her voice that it almost pains me. "I hate sleeping alone."

I squeeze her hand tightly, letting my other hand slide down her cheek to cup her jaw, tilting her face up to mine. My thumb tenderly strokes the pale flesh of her face. Her skin is soft and pristine and perfect. Her eyes scan mine, searching for something. It's been so long since I've been the one another reached out to for comfort. The feeling is uncomfortable and scary and somehow welcomed somewhere deep down. I lean in and lay my lips softly against hers, trying to portray my willingness to be her comfort in the way my mouth molds against hers. Her lips push back against mine. A soft sigh leaves her and breathes life into me. It's tender and vulnerable. A kiss full of things left unsaid.

"I'm not going to leave you, princess," I whisper as our kiss comes to an end. "I'll be right here."

She squeezes my hand back, saying what she needs without saying anything at all. Our fingers interlock and she settles in, holding on to me tightly. She feels so small, so delicate, so breakable. *So entirely mine.*

"How about a movie?"

A smile pulls at the corners of my lips. Snuggling with my girl, and I guess also her cat, sounds like the perfect way to spend an evening.

"You pick the movie, I'll order some dessert," I tell her, hopping out of the bed to dial room service.

"Grab me something chocolatey!" Scarlett hollers at me as she grabs the remote. "Are you good with a scary movie? Maybe Scream or something?"

Turning, I give her a smile. "You're so fucking perfect, princess."

The brunette runs quickly into the room, slamming the door behind her. Shelves crash as she stumbles and tries to right herself. Her breathing is labored, her hair whipping across her face as she searches for the intruder behind her. An eerie silence falls across the room. An atmosphere of impending doom creeps like fog across the screen.

Her shrill shrieks pierce the silence as the Ghostface killer pops up into the window, brandishing a bloodied knife. The black and white mask is emotionless, haunting. Humans rely entirely on facial expressions to read emotions, without them they are lost. Being unable to gauge the emotional response of the person in front of you is the unnerving element of the masked murderer. It's not the mask that scares them, but the lack of being able to understand the person beneath. The brunette screams, shaking her head in horror as the masked man bangs on the glass, desperate to get to her. No facial expressions needed to understand the message he's trying to send her. She's locked in, his perfect prey, destined to find her demise at the end of his blade.

Next to me, Scarlett softly snores through the horror illuminating the darkened room. After eating our fill of chocolate cake and ice cream, with me licking some of the melted sweetness off her while she enjoyed her snack, we snuggled up to watch the movie. She fell asleep almost immediately.

I've barely watched a moment of the film, too enamored with her to look away for more than a few seconds. The soft rise and fall of her chest while she peacefully sleeps is the most comforting thing I've ever felt. Her fingers entwined with mine, grounding me here in the now, fills me with more peace and security than I've felt in a very long time… maybe ever. I could lay here watching her sleep for eternity and not regret a single moment of that time spent with her.

I've been tempted, more than once, to enter her dreams and fuck her senseless. Each time her eyelids flicker, the demon inside me whispers deliciously decadent fantasies I could use to bring her to completion in utterly deplorable ways within her dream space. But I resist. She's been through a lot recently. She needs the rest.

Samson has barely left her side, except to down a little water. He pretends to be asleep but I see him peek a slanted eye open every so often, scanning for anything out of the normal. He's an unusual cat. He seems very attached to my girl. Me, however, he's still on the fence about.

A sudden sharp noise pulls my attention from the sleeping beauty lying next to me. A glow emanates from the bedside table next to her. *Her phone.*

I should leave it be. It's her business. No one likes a nosey and jealous girlfriend…

Fuck it. I'm a jealous and possessive bitch. She fell for me this way, so this is the me she's getting.

Carefully disentangling myself from her, I slip from underneath the blanket. As quietly as I can, I round the bed to inspect her phone.

> **KYLE: Hey. We need to talk. Carnival in 20 minutes. I don't give a shit about what you're doing. Be there or else.**

This motherfucker.

An idea suddenly strikes me. I really don't want to leave my girl, but when an opportunity presents itself, only a fool ignores fate.

SCARLETT: I'll be there.

Shooting off the text to Kyle, I move over to the wardrobe. I dress as quietly as I can, careful not to wake my girl. I promised her I wouldn't leave her. I gave her my word that I would stay by her side. Guilt coils through my core. It's a feeling I haven't felt in a very long time. I don't have a soul, I'm not supposed to feel these types of things. And yet, the nagging sensation of worry pulses through me. I don't want to leave her, but time is running out. If I don't find my thirteenth victim soon, there will be no more nights with her in our future at all. But, if my plan works how I hope it will, she will still be sleeping peacefully when I return and all our problems will be dealt with. I can whisk her away from this shitty town and give her the life she deserves. I want to give her the world, but first I have to deal with her ex.

With a final look back at my beautiful girl, I exit the door to find Kyle.

CHAPTER FIFTEEN

Morgan

The sickening smell of human stench and sugary cotton candy assault my nose as I weave through the crowd of people. Most are already drunk. The lights of the old, rickety rides light up the night sky. This Halloween carnival is the perfect place to meet my lucky victim thirteen. Everyone has a mask covering their face and too much chaos in their veins to worry about anyone other than themselves. I just have to get him alone, maybe behind the fun house or in a carnies trailer and then I can suck him and be done. The macabre madness surrounding me is a fitting scene for Kyle's violent demise.

A twinge of guilt twists within my gut. I don't want to fuck this worthless use of a human meat sack. I want to be feasting on the delicious cunt of my sweet Scarlett. I left her sleeping peacefully, but the knowledge that she might view this as betrayal, as me cheating on her, weighs heavily on me. She asked me not to leave her and yet I did, and to go fuck her ex. I need his soul to survive, but I'm starting to think I won't be able to survive without her either.

It doesn't sit well with me at all but I don't want his pleasure, I want his pain. I think my love would be on board with that after everything he's put her through.

Above us, the blood moon hangs heavy and ominous. Debauchery and mayhem seem to permeate the air. I can sense the lurking danger dripping down the damp fall air.

I have a bad feeling about tonight.

If it wasn't the night of the blood moon, I wouldn't be here. I'd be wrapped up in the arms of my sweet little seductress. Her taste is still thick on my tongue. I never want there to be a time when I can't taste her in my mouth. She has snaked her way around my blackened soul and completely ensnared me. I'm utterly and desperately obsessed with her.

A line of drunken humans is wrapped in a twisted pattern ahead. Fear and anticipation are thick in the air radiating off them. It's intoxicating. If I wasn't on a mission I would stay right here, savoring their stench. They seem to be in line for some type of carousel. As I get closer, I take in the grotesque attraction they're all waiting for. It's a carousel of death. The animals are all in various forms of decomposition, some completely skeletonized. It's a macabre marvel.

Then, I see him. With a beer in one hand, he leans against the fence that surrounds the long tables of the outdoor dining area with a scowl on his face. Kyle is wearing a tight fitting black long-sleeve tee and distressed denim that show off his toned physique. His blonde hair is slicked back and styled to an unnatural degree. He would be attractive, if it wasn't for the dangerous rage radiating off him in waves. His gray eyes scan the crowd with the fierceness of a man looking to cause pain. I've seen that look in a man's eyes before—it never ends well. I say a silent prayer of thanks to the Devil himself that I was able to intercept his text message and keep my princess far away from this evil. The only demon that will be enjoying her from now on will be me. Her pain, her pleasure, her everything is mine.

Blowing out a slow breath, I steel myself to face this man. The knowledge that he's hurt my love causes violent anger to bubble in my gut. The barbs within me prick against the skin of my most delicate area, desperate to unleash their Hellish fury on this dick. I clench and unclench as my pussy pulses in anticipation, ready to be pumped full of blood and cum.

I'm going to savor your pain and feast on your fear, Kyle.

I sway my hips in a seductive swing. The blood-red, leather, bandage dress I have on fits me like a glove. It's wrapped around my body like a second skin. My heavy eye make-up and dark lipstick add to my alluring appearance. As I walk, people stare. Eyes assess me, taking in my attractive exterior. But it's not for them. I'm here to catch just one fly in my web.

"Kyle, right?" His eyes swiftly shift to me as I grab his attention. I skim my sharpened nails lightly up his bicep.

It takes him a moment. He looks at my face, clearly trying to place me.

You really face fuck so many random women behind seedy clubs that you forgot the one from just this week, asshole?

"You're the girl from the bar," realization spreads across his face. A smirk pulls at the corner of his lips, exposing his whitened teeth. His canines glint in the strobing lights of the carnival. He leans in conspiratorially before whispering, "The one who let me fuck her tight little throat in an alleyway."

The one whose soul I tried to suck through his cock before I fucked his woman, is more accurate, but semantics I suppose.

"I thought that looked like you." My breasts press up against him as I wrap my arm around his bicep, spinning my web further around my precious prey. "Are you here with someone?" I let my lips caress the shell of his ear as I speak to him. He shivers as my warm breath brushes against his skin. "I'd hate to keep you from them if you are."

He looks down at me and I can see the maddening lust swirling in his blown out pupils.

Caught you, Kyle.

"No one," he mumbles as he grinds his core against me. I can feel his thickening cock push against my stomach.

"So you're free then?" I discreetly slip my hand between us, letting my fingers glide across the hard length beneath his jeans. He moans against me as I rub up and down ever so softly, just enough to drive him wild.

"Want to go back to my place?" His words come out mumbled as his breathing is jagged and desperate. He runs his nose along the column of my bared neck.

"I saw a spot behind the fun house. Maybe we could just go there?" I offer, trying to be as discreet as possible and not draw extra attention our way. I grab his thick length and squeeze the head, earning a growl from him as his lips suck against my neck. I immediately pull away.

He can't leave a single mark that Scarlett will see. She can't think I'd willingly let anyone other than her touch me.

He pauses, looking angry at my resistance. Fuck, I need to keep him on the hook. I *need* this. I'm too close to the deadline. I've never let it go on this long before without claiming all thirteen victims. I can't let my deal with the Devil be broken or it will be me headed to Hell instead of Kyle. I *need* his soul and I need it tonight.

I bat my lashes and attempt to look as seductive and sweet as possible. "I don't think I can wait to get back to your place," I pin my lip between my teeth. His eyes track the movement. "I want you now."

Lust and need flame in his eyes. The desire to claim, possess, and ruin is clearly his intent. His eyes fall to my breasts and I can practically see him drooling.

Typical fucking human male.

"Let me just text my friend and let them know I'm going to be a minute."

And by friend, you mean your long-term girlfriend, you were supposed to meet up with in order to fix things? What a real fucking prince you are, Kyle.

I step back from him. He slides his phone out of his pocket and quickly clicks away. His cock is evidently ready, bulging against the tight denim of his jeans, hardened with need. Finishing his message, he slides his phone back in his pocket and returns his sinister stare toward me.

"Come on, babe." I hold out my hand to him and when his thick palm lands in mine, we're off.

I lead him through the crowd, weaving around drunken fools and scandalously dressed women. The smell of human sin is in the air tonight. I draw in a deep breath, savoring the debauchery. I'm going to suck Kyle's soul then go back to the hotel room and fuck my girl until she's so delirious, she won't even remember his name. The anticipation is exquisite. My nipples harden beneath my dress.

The funhouse is a grotesque monstrosity pitched against the evening sky. It's a looming mask of a creepy as fuck clown. Its open mouth is a darkened tunnel leading inside. The eyes of the clown are downturned slightly, creating a sinister expression. Screams peel through the air from within. The red glow of the ancient lights cast an eerie haze across the darkened night sky.

This is where Kyle meets his end.

Rounding the back of the funhouse, my figure barely reaches the shadows before I'm roughly shoved up against the broken wooden wall. My face hits the surface with a harsh thud. Teeth, tongues, lips, and fingers are everywhere. Touching, pulling, licking, hurting.

"Wait—" I begin before his hand grabs the back of my neck. He shoves my head roughly against the wall again. Pain shoots through my skull, radiating out from the spot where my temple made contact with the wall.

Fingers find my panties and roughly shove them to the side before assaulting my poor pussy.

"You wet for me, slut?" His stale beer breath wafts down onto my face as he speaks.

Dry as a fucking desert, dude.

"Yeah, baby." I give him my best fake moan, hoping he's drunk enough not to notice that my body is not responding to him.

"I'm going to have you screaming my name so loudly all the people at this shitty little carnival will hear you."

Doubtful.

I need to do something to help. I need to fuck him. I need to dig my teeth into his cock, shred him to pieces and suck his soul. And I need it *now.*

I close my eyes and picture my princess on her knees for me. I think about those big, soulful brown eyes staring up at me with such innocent purity as she sticks out her tongue and tastes me. I think about sliding my fingers into her silky locks and pulling her sweet little lips onto my cunt.

That does the trick. My pussy begins to weep as I envision my girl.

"That's it baby, you like that huh?" He thrusts a thick digit roughly inside me. I gasp at the sudden intrusion. "I'm going to stretch this pussy nice and wide to take my massive cock."

Calm down, I've already seen it and it's nothing to write home about.

"Please," I whine. "Please, fuck me. I need your big fat cock in me right now."

A sinister voice slivers across the exposed skin of my shoulders, causing goosebumps to erupt. "Oh, you'll get what you came for you stupid fucking slut. But first, we're going to take a walk."

A click pierces the quiet air of the autumn night. The cold press of metal against my skin has a shiver running down my spine. *A gun. He has a fucking gun.* I turn my head as slowly as possible, careful not to make any sudden movements as a looming shadow peers down at me.

"This is the friend you were texting?" I direct my question at Kyle, who has now disentangled himself from me, and is standing next to his friend.

"*Evil lurks within his soul,*" the demon's voice calls from the depths of my soulless consciousness.

"We thought we'd all have a little fun. Just the three of us." The man approaches me, his fingers sliding around my neck and squeezing. I keep my face neutral, trying to remain as calm as possible. He's the same man from the club when I first met Kyle. His evil eyes are ones I won't forget. This man thinks he just caught a weak little plaything to torture for the night. Little does he know, he's not the predator.

I rip myself away from his grip. His touch burns. "And what if I have no interest in your sad, shriveled little cock?"

The pain isn't immediate. It takes a moment to register the throbbing ache that seems to rip my skull in half as he pistol-whips me. The world spins and swirls as I try to regain my composure. Bile rises in my throat.

"Tie her fucking arms," he demands and before I can react, my wrists are yanked behind my back and bound with rope.

They brought rope and a gun? These motherfuckers planned to rape a girl tonight. Too bad for them, they picked the wrong female to fuck with.

Looking up into the eyes of evil, I feel the demon try to escape. He wants to rip this fuckers throat out and make sure he can never hurt another person ever again. His evil exists entirely to cause pain, as if he feeds off it. A true monster.

"Let's walk."

I go willingly. Not because I'm weak. Not because I'm afraid. No, I walk away from the comforting lights of the carnival and the voices of the people reveling in debauchery, because I want the space and time I need in order to enjoy my meal. I'm going to savor sucking their fucking souls out of their human forms and sending these two assholes straight to the pits of Hell.

I only need one soul, but I'll willing kill both these fuckers. And, I'll enjoy every moment of it.

They lead me further and further into the fields. The lights and sounds of the carnival grow further and further away until it's just an eerie whisper left on the wind. My heels dig into the soft soil beneath us as we weave through rows of decaying and rotting pumpkins. The blood-red moon sits high in the sky above us, bathing the entire world in a red glow.

When we reach the far end of the field, I'm unceremoniously thrown to the ground. My knees squish into the mud and decaying flesh of unpicked gourds. The smell is assaulting, like overripe earth. The rain stopped earlier but a moist mist still clings to the orange skin of the pumpkins surrounding us. The drops of dew glisten in the moonlight. My head throbs where I was hit and the tender flesh of my wrists stings beneath the rope. I keep my head down, my long hair acting like a curtain around my face. It hides the sinister smirk that pulls across my lips as I smile at the pumpkin beneath me, thinking of how sweet this agony will be.

Pain for pain and blood for blood, boys.

"What's the plan here, Will?" Kyle asks as they both

circle me like hungry sharks.

"You caught her so you get first go, but I'm going to film. 'Whore fucked in pumpkin patch' has a nice ring to it don't you think? I'll snap a pic of her tear-streaked face in the dirt. It'll be great click-bait for the site."

My eyes fly up to the men above me. I can feel the demon within trying to burst to the surface, craving to rip these two shit sacks to pieces, but I will him back down. I need a cock in me first. Then I can unleash Hell.

"You two assholes rape women and film it to put online?" I can't help the disgust in my tone.

Will leans down, the smell of vodka radiates off him in waves. His black button-down is open slightly at the neck, exposing tanned skin. His dirty blonde hair is styled out of his face, leaving his chiseled features exposed. He's attractive, alluring even, but his eyes tell a different story. They're dark pools of rage and hatred. Evil recognizes evil, and in him, I see nothing but darkness. He might not have sold his soul to the Devil, but he clearly belongs in Hell.

"Yes, and you're going to make me so much money. With this pretty face," his long and lean fingers stroke my cheek, landing on my chin and pulling my face up to examine me further. I sit up as he pulls me onto my knees. "These epic tits," he reaches down and violently rips my dress down, exposing my breasts. The cool night air caresses my nipples, making them stiffen. "And this tight little cunt," his hand snakes further down, finding my bare lips.

He rubs the outside of my pussy gently, almost lovingly. I can feel myself dampen with pleasure as he finds my clit and strokes soft circles around the hardening bud.

"Such a good little slut for us, aren't you?" His strokes become faster and I can't stop the moan of pleasure that escapes my lips. "Not even wearing panties for us?"

He pinches my clit lightly and I feel pleasure curl in my core. He goes back to soft, circular movements as my desire builds. The cool night air wraps around my exposed breasts. The heat, the cold, and the pain are almost too much, and yet somehow not quite enough. I feel myself edging closer and closer to the precipes of pleasure with each stroke of his fingers.

"Please," I moan as he works me with expert precision.

And then he stops. I stare up at him in anger as he rises back to his full height.

"You want to come? Then do it on camera."

This motherfucker.

Kyle approaches me next, weaving his hand in my hair and yanking my head back. My eyes stare up at the blood moon above us as I hear his zipper being lowered. He brings the soft head of his cock to my mouth and I willingly open for him. He's gentle at first, letting his length skim across the flat surface of my awaiting tongue. I lick at each ridge of the veins on his cock as he moans in pleasure.

"You suck cock so fucking good, baby."

Only had a few centuries of practice to nail down my technique, but thanks, asshole.

"Pull her hair and fuck her face," Will demands from behind us. I shift my eyes to his darkened form and see him slip his phone out of his pocket. The camera light blinds me momentarily as he illuminates the scene. "The audience loves to see them cry. Make her choke on your cock until she's begging for you to fuck her pussy and give her throat a break."

Kyle obliges. His fingers roughly tug at my hair, stinging my scalp. He shoves his hard length in as deep as it can go, causing me to choke and splutter around his cock. My nose hits his pelvic bone with a thud. The coarse hair of his crotch scratches my face.

"Fuck baby, this throat feels too fucking good," he grunts as he ruthlessly fucks my face. I watch Will through my periphery. His phone is aimed right at us, filming us. Despite my best attempts to not give them what they want, tears prick the corners of my eyes. "You like swallowing my fat fucking cock, you dirty slut?"

I'll like it more when it's ripped from your body and I use the dismembered organ as a toy to fuck your girlfriend.

He pulls out of me and I greedily suck in air. Spit hangs between my mouth and his length, shimmering in the moonlight. I pant and try to regain my composure as they chuckle.

"Please," I manage between gasps. "Please, fuck me."

The barbs within me pulse, ready to devour. Ready to consume his soul and finish this.

Kyle looks down at me with a satisfied sneer. "You want to cream around my cock, slut?"

"Please," I beg again, shimmying in the dirt so my tits bob slightly. His eyes track the movement and his dick twitches in my face.

Caught you Kyle.

"Turn around and bend over," he demands. I try to comply. It's difficult with my arms still tied behind my back. Using the rope for leverage, he holds my bound wrists in one hand, bending me over and pulling my dress up over my ass with the other.

A sharp smack cracks through the crisp air. The tender flesh of my ass stings. He lands a second smack, this time on my other cheek. "Look at this thick fucking ass," he croons as he rubs the spot he just slapped. "Maybe when I'm done using your pussy, I'll fuck this tight little asshole." His finger finds my puckered hole and presses against the entrance. I shriek and try to pull away. That's not where I need him.

"Maybe, if you're a very good girl," Will's voice carries across the darkened ground to where I'm bent over and at their mercy. "We'll fuck both your slutty little holes at once. You want us both to fuck you?"

Now there's an idea.

"Yes," I moan as I grind my ass back against Kyle's hand.

"Such a desperate cock whore, aren't you?" A third slap stings the flesh of my ass. I relish the pain, the filth, the complete and utter desperation of this moment.

Without warning Kyle slams into me from behind, his cock stuffing me full. I scream out into the night at the sudden intrusion. He pounds into me ruthlessly, taking everything and giving nothing in return. His fingers dig into the flesh of my hips, pulling me closer with every thrust.

"Fuck, that's it slut. You like being split in half by my cock?"

The pain morphs into pleasure as the barbs move towards the surface of my inner walls. My muscles clench in anticipation of the feast.

Warmth swarms in my core, drawing me closer and closer to desire. My nipples are hard and aching to be touched. I want so badly to bring my hand down to my core and flick my throbbing clit, but I'm still restrained. He rips at my flesh tightly, my back to his front as he pounds into me with wild abandon like a fucking beast.

"Tell me how good this cock feels, baby," he demands, leaning in to whisper against the side of my face. Will moves in front of us, filming the entire time. I can see his hardened length tenting his pants from here.

"You know that saying 'Hell hath no fury like a woman scorned,' Kyle?" I speak to him as my eyes stare straight into the camera. I let the mask start to fall. I can sense my eyes shifting and the pupils expanding. The sclera recedes so all that's left is blackened midnight tinged with blood red.

"The fuck are you on about?" Kyle grunts out between each punishing pound of his hips, completely oblivious to the trap he's fallen into. His cock twitches as he thrusts again and again into my pussy. He's close, I can sense it.

"What the fuck is wrong with you?" Will's voice is fearful. His terror is delicious. It's like fresh honey stuck to my tongue. So fucking sweet. But Kyle ignores him, too delirious with the need to finish to notice he's about to die.

"I'm a furious fucking woman, Kyle," I drive my hips back roughly, pleasure pulsing through my dripping pussy. "And this cock is exactly what I've been waiting for to fuel my fury."

His cock twitches as my pussy spasms. We're both so fucking close.

"Shut the fuck up bitch and take my fucking cock."

"With pleasure."

I fall over the edge. My orgasm rips through me like a blazing fire. Wave after wave of ecstasy pulses through my entire body. I scream out into the night. I can't hold back anymore. My tongue expands, splitting in two and slithers like snakes from between my lips. Will screams, falling to the ground on his ass. His phone flies from his hand, landing off among the rotting corpses of pumpkins. I can taste both men's fear and desire as I flick my forked tongue.

It's delicious. It fuels my orgasm further, causing my walls to contract again and again.

"Fuck!" Kyle falls over the edge with me while Will sits on his ass in utter horror, watching as I begin to drag pleasure out of Kyle's cock.

With the first burst of his warm cum inside me, I fully let go and release. The barbs break loose, shifting from inside me and piercing Kyle's pulsing length. My sharpened teeth break through skin and tendon, ripping into him and burrowing within. Sticky blood and cum bursts from him, covering my insides with delicious warmth.

Kyle screams and shrieks. His pain and panic makes this all that more exquisite.

"Oh yeah, baby, scream for me," I croon as I suck more and more on his bloodied cock.

I can't hold it any longer, the mask falls entirely, revealing my true demonic form. Horns sprout from beneath my hair. Dark lines snake along the length of my limbs as my veins turn inky black. My fingers lengthen and my nails turn to claws. The beast is unleashed.

"Get her the fuck off of me!" Kyle screams at Will. But the other man is completely frozen in utter horror as he takes in the sight in front of him. Kyle's shrieks turn to moans as I milk more cum out of him, taking everything he's got.

"What the fuck?!" Will screams, as he scoots backwards on his hands and ass.

Each drop of Kyle's soul is delicious. It fuels me and fills me. Warmth floods my entire being, slithering through my darkened veins and nourishing the demon within. My thirteenth victim was worth the fucking wait.

Having drunk almost every single drop of his soul, I release him. My teeth recede back beneath the surface of my pussy walls, allowing him to fall to the dirt with a thud. I rip my arms apart violently, breaking the ties that bind me and freeing my hands. I right my skirt, pull my leather dress back over my tits, then stand to my full height. I spin to look down at Kyle's dying, useless body laying in the mud. His eyes widen to the size of saucers, taking in my demonic form glowing in the light of the blood moon. I watch as he struggles to take his last few dying breaths.

Cocking my head to the side, I let a sinister smile spread across my face. He deserves this torture for the pain he inflicted on others.

Karma's a bitch, Kyle. And so am I.

"Oh, and Kyle," I crouch down, making sure he hears this with his last dying breaths. I dip my finger into the bloody mess of mutilated flesh that was his dick. Bringing his warm and sticky blood to my lips, I slip my finger into my mouth, moaning at the taste of his violent death on my tongue. I turn my eyes to meet his before rising back to my full height. "I stole your girlfriend. I'm going to leave here and fuck her until she doesn't even remember your name while you die sad and alone in the dirt."

I need him to know that he lost her before he passes on to Hell.

The cock of a gun behind me pulls my attention. I spin to see Will standing and dusting himself off, pointing the barrel of his gun at me.

"What the fuck are you?!" he shouts, trying desperately to not sound as frightened as he is. I can taste his fear, it's pungent. He can't hide from me.

I take a step towards him. In my true form I'm much closer to his height. He's not as opposing when he's facing someone his own size. Still, the gun is a bit of a problem.

"What's wrong Will? You don't want to play anymore?" I stalk closer to him, enjoying playing with my next meal.

"Stay the fuck away from me or I'll fucking shoot you! I'm not fucking kidding!" He raises the gun higher, aiming straight for my heart.

"No!" A scream rips through the quiet of the air and a flash of white dances in the periphery of my vision.

My heart falls. Fear like I've never known before suffocates me as I watch her petite form launch itself from behind a tree and shoot towards Will. Scarlett leaps at the monster in front of us, pulling his attention off of me for a split second as they struggle with the gun.

And then a shot rings out through the darkness of the night.

CHAPTER SIXTEEN

Scarlett

The sound of the gun is so loud that I'm temporarily deaf. All I can hear is ringing. The world spins on its axis as I try to right myself while looking around to figure out what just happened. Hands land around my throat before I have time to gather myself. My vision goes in and out. Black spots dance around the periphery of sight. The ringing continues, blurring out the sounds of the outside world. Everything feels slowed down, as if the world has stopped, just for this moment.

All I know is that I have to fight. I can't leave Morgan. I need to get to her. To help her. I can't lose her.

I saw what she is—a *demon*.

And I don't care. I love her. Demon or not, she's beautiful and she makes me feel like no one else ever has. I'm going to fight for her, for us. I'm not losing her. She's mine and I'm hers. These motherfuckers aren't ruining that for us.

I kick and scratch and claw until the pressure on my throat slackens enough for me to greedily suck in air. My eyes shoot open to be assaulted by the horror surrounding me.

Kyle lays on the ground near me. His vacant eyes stare unblinkingly at me. Blood stains his skin. He's very clearly dead. His face is twisted into a look of grotesque shock. It's a horrific sight and yet I feel...nothing.

Yes, I feel physical pain radiating through my entire body. But as I look at the man I thought I once loved, lying violently mutilated and murdered on the ground, I can't force myself to feel the anger and pain I know that I should feel. Instead, I just feel...empty.

A sharp slap to my cheek pulls me from my thoughts. "Scarlett, what the fuck? That thing is a fucking monster. She killed Kyle! Get your shit together and let's go!"

Kyle's friend Will straddles me, a gun in one hand and his other still lightly against my throat. Above him, the blood moon hangs ominously in the night sky, casting a gruesome glow across the world. Will looks down at me with a hot anger radiating off of him. His fingers are swollen and scratched from where I clawed at him while he strangled me. Right after he shot—

My eyes frantically dart around the shadow streaked ground, desperately searching for my goddess. When I finally spot her, my entire world darkens. She's lying lifeless on the ground. Her chest isn't rising and falling like it should. She lays on the ground behind Kyle, just as silent and unmoving as he is.

Will's hand snakes into my hair, pulling me to my feet. "Why the fuck are you here anyway, Scarlett? Were you following your boyfriend like a nosey bitch? Or are you here for something else?"

"Fuck you and fuck him too. You're both assholes. I'm here for her. She's worth more than the two of you could ever amount to in your entire lives." The words lighten something in me. I've been holding on to so much hurt and pain caused by Kyle, I didn't even know it was weighing me down.

His hand leaves my hair to strike my face again. The sting is sharp as the back of his hand connects with my cheek. My head snaps to the side and I stumble. I almost trip on Kyle as I try to keep myself upright. Next to him the ground is barren. My goddess is gone.

"She bewitched you with her demon cunt and turned you gay? Are you that fucking dumb, you stupid bitch?" Will moves to grab me again, his monstrous form looms like a shadow of rage and hate. "Maybe I should take you with me and remind you that the entire purpose of your cunt is to accept and please cock."

This misogynistic asshole is getting his dick nowhere near me.

But he has a gun and I have nothing.

"If you get your filthy cock anywhere near my princess, I will slit you from ear to anus and feast on your entrails." The voice that slithers slowly from the shadows of the woods is filled with the promise of deadly female venom.

My goddess stalks from the shadows into the haunting light of the blood moon. Only now, she's changed. Dark and rough horns rise from out of her golden locks, curling towards the back of her head. She's taller; her limbs are longer and her nails are sharp shiny talons. Her eyes are black pits, completely empty of any white. Red streaks of lightning pulse in the onyx orbs. Her skin is paler, and dark black veins snake beneath the surface. She's a beautiful nightmare. My goddess of death and destruction.

Will spins, aiming the gun straight at her heart. The heart that belongs to me.

"You're just some stupid fucking chick! I'm not—"

"Afraid of me?" My goddess stalks closer towards her prey. Waves of viscous power radiate from her being. "You should be William, you really should be afraid of this woman."

"Don't come a step closer or I'll shoot!" he shrieks, cocking the gun and holding it with an unsteady hand.

Fear courses through me like fire. My heart thunders inside my chest as I desperately watch the scene unfolding in front of me. He can't shoot her. I won't let him. She is mine and I'm not letting this asshole take her from me tonight.

"Will!" I scream at him, my shrill voice bouncing between

the trees and echoing through the emptiness of the night.

He whips around to face me. I paint a pained expression on my face, letting him see the weak little girl I was before I met Morgan. It's the distraction my lady needs. Her red talons slice across his neck, becoming deep scarlet pools on his skin beneath her touch.

"You fucking bitches!" He hollers, whirling toward Morgan and slamming his fists at her. He's quick—she's quicker.

With grace unlike anything I've ever seen before, she dodges each of his blows with ease. His shoulders are hunched in anger and white wisps escape his lips as he angrily screams into the darkness of the night.

"I knew something was wrong with you the moment I saw you! I should have fucked you and disposed of you that first night in the alleyway, before you brought corruption and chaos here." He spits at her between heaving breaths, exhausted from trying to catch her.

"Oh fuck off with this whole 'the Devil makes people gay' shit. The Devil is too busy feasting on souls to give a shit where you stick your cock."

With Will momentarily stunned by my goddesses' sassy mouth, she takes the opportunity to pounce. Her razor sharp talons slice through his shirt, leaving shredded fabric and skin hanging across his front. Then the blood comes. Red rivulets ooze from the gashes, staining his skin and running like rivers down his form. His hands grasp at his mutilated flesh. It's only then I notice he's no longer holding the gun.

"Threaten my girl again Will and I'll slice your cock from your body…slowly."

He pales and falls to his knees. The soft ground beneath him sinks, pulling him down to the Earth. I turn my eyes to my goddess to see her eyes assessing me critically.

"I'm fine," I assure her as I begin to move towards her.

She takes a few steps towards me, a smile crossing her lips and the tension easing from her shoulders as she takes in my unharmed state. Suddenly she falters and she falls.

I run to her, catching her as she collapses completely. "Morgan?" I cradle her limp figure as she tries, unsuccessfully, to hold her head upright.

Her body looks so limp and fragile lying motionless on the cold earth. I hold onto her core, trying to figure out what the hell is happening. My hands skim down her form until I reach a damp patch on her stomach. Pulling my hand back I realize in horror that blood is seeping from her core. The blood red of her dress covered the stain.

I didn't even see her pain as she fought to protect me. "What the fuck happened?"

"The gun, babe," her voice is so much weaker than I've ever heard it. "You need to get out of here. Run."

"I'm not leaving you—"

"You have to run. You need to get away from him and

get somewhere safe."

Will's not a threat anymore. In the pale light of the moon I can see his figure slinking through the twirling veins of the pumpkin patch, running away like the bitch he is.

"He's gone. Come on, let's go and find help." I try my best to hold her weight and pull us up, but her anguished cry stops me.

"You have to let me go, Scarlett."

The pain in her eyes is enough to break me. It's as if I can see my life on a linear plane, laid out in front of me in that moment—everything that has been and will be.

"There's no life for me without you, Morgan. I love you. You make me strong and brave and confident. I have become the me I've always wanted to be, because of you. You can't leave me now. I love you."

"Scarlett, I'm no one's knight in shining armor. Just look at me," she motions weakly to the horns still protruding from her head. "I'm the villain of this tale."

"Then be my villain, and let me love you just how you are."

Her eyes go wide and empty, her stare fixed on something behind me. I know it's him before I even turn to see him. The stench of decay hangs thickly in the air, the pungent smell assaulting my senses. The air turns freezing, my breath escaping my mouth in puffs of frigid white. All light seems to have been snuffed out, extinguished by his presence.

Slowly, I turn to meet his unseeing gaze. His dark

hood and cloak masks his form in blackened shadows. An apparition of darkness. Here yet not truly of this world, he seems to swim through the night air towards us. I can't see his eyes but I can feel them assessing me as he approaches. I cling tighter to Morgan's limp body.

"You can't have her," I state, sounding far more confident than I feel.

He doesn't respond. He doesn't need to. Death bends to no man.

But I'm not a man.

"Please, I love her. My life without her will be shades of gray. She's my light, my color, my vibrancy and joy. Please do not take her from me."

He cocks his hooded head. Clearly the pleas of a poor girl amuse the Ruler of the Dead.

"If you take her, then take me too. I will not let you take her from me. She's *mine*. I claim her."

If Death could laugh he would. And yet, he's not taking her. He seems to be considering my request. His black cloaked hand motions to my arm. He doesn't need to say a word, I know what he asks of me. I place my palm to the sky and hold out my arm, exposing the pale expanse of my arm to him. My purple veins seem to glow brightly beneath my alabaster skin. I'd willingly drain each and every vein, pull my heart from my chest, give my soul, anything he asked and more—for her. I'd happily die if it meant an eternity with my Morgan.

With a final glance, he asks without any words. I nod in agreement. I'm ready.

Searing pain like I've never known pierces my skin. It burns and stings like a thousand tiny needles all on fire, scorching through my skin and tendons. I scream and shriek as my vision becomes blinded by white hot agony. But I don't pull my arm back. As much as I want the pain to stop, I want her more. The sensation of being torn in two spreads up my arm and into my mind. It's as if my entire being is being ripped in half. Torturous radiating pain shoots through every single piece of me.

And then as suddenly as it started, it all stops.

I'm left breathing heavy. My body stooped and sagging under the weight of what just happened. The shock wears off and I start to shiver in the cold night air. I feel like I might be sick. The pain recedes slowly, everything returning to normal. Everything except my arm.

Emblazoned in dark black ink is a swirling symbol on the inside of my lower arm, right beneath my inner elbow. It's dark and intricate and striking. Its beauty is strangely familiar.

"Mine," her breath is barely audible, her voice almost gone. But it's her. My goddess is alive.

I wrap my arms around her tightly, holding her against my chest. Her heart beats against me, it's thumping enough to cause tears to fall in waves over my cheeks. I sob into her hair as we both hold onto each other for what feels like an eternity.

"You offered yourself for me?" she finally asks, her voice regaining some of its former fire.

I pull back to meet her eyes. She searches my face with such open vulnerability that it almost breaks me. How could she not realize that I'd do anything for her?

"Of course," I brush a soft piece of her silken hair behind her ear before laying a chaste kiss to her plush lips. "I can't live without you. I'm yours, remember?"

"Scarlett, I'm a demon. That symbol on your arm— that's the symbol of the Hell demon inhabiting my soul," she pushes up to sitting, her hand cradling my cheek. "You didn't just offer your life for me love, you sold your soul."

Hearing it put into words causes my mouth to go dry and my palms to sweat. A deal with the Devil sounds… *intense*. But I don't regret a thing. For her, I'd sell everything I have and all I ever will be.

"I'd sell my soul to the Devil a thousand times over to save you, to be with you."

She rises to her full height, standing over me like the imposing demon goddess she is. The blood moon illuminates the sky above her, surrounding her head like a halo from Hell. She is beauty and power, sun and seduction, my savior and my villain.

"You didn't sell your soul to the Devil, my love. You sold it to me. It's my mark on you. Me who owns your beautiful soul," her hand shoots out, her talons gripping my chin. "You're mine, from now until eternity, princess."

"I'm yours? Truly?"

A smile spreads across her face. She nods, acknowledging that I've truly found my other half, even if I had to sell my soul to do it. Her smile warms my core, filling me with more joy than I've ever felt in my life before now.

"You're mine, Scarlett, for the rest of our lives. And when your soul embarks this existence I shall follow you into the darkness beyond. You're mine now, and for all the eternities that come afterwards."

The weight of her words hits me hard. I'm hers. Maybe I should be afraid, but I'm not. The pain of the night has faded and now I just feel…whole.

"Ready, my love?" she asks, holding her hand out for me. I take one look back—back at the corpse of the man I thought I loved and the life I had lived before, a life that was not worth living. Turning back to the woman I truly love, I reach out and grab her hand in return. She pulls me to my feet and kisses me lightly on the forehead.

"What about Will?" I ask her as we step over Kyle's lifeless body and head back towards the lights and noise of the carnival ahead.

"He's gone for now. But he will find his way to Hell, I can sense it."

I give her a quizzical look but find her staring at my arm,

at the new mark left there. She looks proud and pleased to see me marked as hers.

"Let's go home. Samson must be worried sick about you." Her slender fingers slip between mine, holding my hand tightly. Our pulses thrum against one another as we walk slowly through the decaying gourds and soft earth. Covered head to toe in mud and blood, we walk off into our new life—together and in love.

EPILOGUE

Morgan

I've been sitting at this shitty bar for what feels like ages. Stalking is certainly not for the impatient. My intel told me they'd be here though, at this bar, tonight. I just have to bide my time and wait for my prey.

I swirl the amber liquid in my glass, watching the waves crash along the pale sand of the pristine beach. The wall of windows behind the bar gives me the perfect view of the Florida coast. It's hot, humid, and sticky. Beads of perspiration slip down the side of my glass in twisted rivulets as the ice in my Scotch slowly melts away. Fuck Florida. I'm growing very sick of being in this hell hole as I try to track him down. This place is an endless pit of alligators and sticky air. I'm ready to leave and head home, but first I have someone to take care of. He's good at hiding in the public eye, I'll give him that. But tonight is the perfect opportunity for me to get what I came here for. I always catch my prey.

A petite brunette enters the bar alone, looking sexy as fuck in a tight little black dress. She's slender and slight with small curves. She looks good enough to eat.

Behind the girl a man enters, his hand sliding across her lower back as he leads her to a private table in the back. He's tall and tanned with salt and pepper hair and a well-fitting blue suite. His Rolex and impeccably put together look screams wealth, money, and power. I'm so glad to see that my prey has in fact entered the establishment, and with a tasty little treat on his arm, too.

"*Mine,*" the demon whispers across the vast expanses of my mind as his focus hones in on the couple crossing the bar. He's becoming insatiable since we almost died a few months back.

A smile pulls at the corner of my mouth as I think about how much fun we're all going to be having tonight. I down my Scotch and slink off the stool I've been sitting on. Swaying my hips seductively and flipping my shimmering golden hair across my shoulder, I step with purpose and determination. My sights set on the couple canoodling in the back corner, oblivious to the danger headed their way.

His arm is thrown over the back of the booth behind her as he leans in, his figure surrounding her in a possessive stance. He's whispering in her ear something that makes her pale cheeks flush red. The red on her skin looks sinfully delicious. She's a vision. He, on the other hand, is an asshole. The ring on his left hand is all I need to confirm that this Florida state senator is exactly the type of man his wife suspects him to be—an unfaithful asshole who is using his position of power to convince young women to fuck him. His wife is paying me well to get these answers for her, and even more for making sure his infidelities are no longer something she has to worry about.

"*Perfect prey,*" the beast within purrs, anticipating our next delicious meal. He looks powerful and vivacious. His soul will be such a treat to consume.

The girl giggles at something he says, her eyes fixated on me. Jealousy rips through me and I struggle to keep my face neutral.

Naughty girl is going to get punished for this.

Approaching the table, I make sure to keep my eyes on his hands and exactly how high they are traveling up her very exposed thighs. *Too exposed.* If I was a worse woman I'd tie her to my bed naked and never let her leave. But she'd insisted on helping. So here we are. I'm not sure I'm enjoying this game as much as she seems to be, though. I will absolutely be punishing her later for this. I'm keeping a tally in my mind of every place his hands touch her pristine skin. Later, I'll need to remind her exactly who owns her body and soul for all eternity.

Then his hand brushes across her pale arm. "That's an interesting tattoo," he comments about the symbol emblazoned on her arm.

Mine.

If the man wasn't already on my kill list, he certainly is now.

Slinking into the booth, I startle the man who disentangles himself from my girl. My hand reaches out instantly to touch her, to remind us both that she's mine and I'm hers. I stroke the symbol on her arm. My symbol.

"You two look like you're down to have a little fun," I speak directly to the man, letting him think he's in charge. He has no idea that he's fallen right into the trap of not one, but two predators.

Leaning my arm on the table, I let him catch a glimpse of my ample cleavage peeking out from beneath my low cut sundress. I can feel Scarlett's eyes assessing me as well. I specifically wore her favorite dress tonight. She says it makes me look sweet. I'm not sure a Hell demon is *sweet*, but I like her praise and attention so I let it be. The man can't pull his eyes off of my tits, he's entranced, practically drooling on the fucking table.

I let my other hand caress her outer thigh under the table. Goosebumps erupt across her skin. *So fucking reactive to my lightest little touch.* If she wants to play games, then we will play. I've been doing this much longer than she has. She'll be begging me to end him quickly so I can fuck her without distraction as soon as we enter the room I've already reserved in the hotel upstairs.

"We are having a good time," the man's hand briefly swipes against mine as we both caress the thighs of the girl between us. "But I'm always open to a party." The sinister smirk he flashes me is pure sin.

"Your girlfriend is very pretty." I push some of Scarlett's hair behind her ear and let the backs of my knuckles caress the column of her delicate little throat.

"My *date* for the evening is very eager to please." He emphasizes the word as if convincing us all that this is just a hookup. No convincing needed here, I am more than happy to dine and dash.

The plan was for Scarlett and I to seduce him together, but my lovely girl ran into him while out grabbing coffee last week and took the opportunity to strike up a conversation with our mark, *my* mark, without me. He's been pursuing her ever since, desperate to sink his dirty dick into her tight little cunt and claim what is rightfully mine. If I hadn't already been contracted to kill the fucker, I'd kill him for the filthy messages he's been sending to my princess.

Why do human men think that all females want to see terribly angled pictures of their cocks? At least women make the effort to pose and look attractive when they send nudes, men just click and send. Fucking pigs.

"Would your date possibly be interested in partying with me tonight?" I ask him instead of her. I already know her answer. I can feel her desire radiating off. If I stuck my hand between her thighs right now I'd find her soaked. My girl is such a good little slut, always ready for me.

"You're more interested in her than me? Are you a fucking dyke or something?" The man's laughter is cruel and biting, his words laced with misogynistic condescension that makes my fucking blood boil. He swigs from his drink as he laughs, completely oblivious to the tension now racking through Scarlett's body. Her eyes swiftly dart to the steak knife on the table. Such a violent little thing my Hellish whore has become. I softly place my hand on top of hers, a reminder that we need to go through with the plan. This night will end in blood and sex, just not in the middle of a crowded hotel bar.

"Or something," I confirm with a nod, eating up every inch of Scarlett's exquisite form with my eyes. And I mean it, the hunger I feel for her hasn't faded at all in the last few months, if anything, I crave her more.

"Maybe you need a big, fat cock to remind you how good it feels to be filled by a man."

My eyes slide to the man on the other side of the booth, assessing his heated gaze. He thinks this will work out for him, that we will bow to his manliness and become cock slaves. *Such a fucking idiot.*

"Maybe I do," I offer him a sly smile, as if his offer is appealing. "Are you offering, *daddy*?"

Scarlett's eyebrows shoot up at the implication. I wonder if she likes me playing the submissive sweetie for a change. Usually I dominate her but men don't want to be dominated, they want a good girl. I undoubtedly have centuries on this man, but he can play daddy for a moment if it'll get the job done. And my girl will get a front row seat to the show.

"Do you have a room here?" the male inquires.

With a nod of my head and a flirtatious pull of my lip between my teeth, I slide my fingers through Scarlett's and lead her out of the booth. Hand in hand, I guide her through the bar. A quick peek over my shoulder ensures the man is behind us, his hungry gaze following every soft sway of our hips. We all pile into the elevator and the moment the doors close, I shove Scarlett against the wall. I can't wait another moment to get my hands on her. I hold her by the hips, possessively digging my fingers into her flesh, as I ravage her mouth. Our chests and cores caress each other as I kiss her up against the mirrored wall. Each swipe of her tongue against mine drives me crazier and crazier.

"Fuck, yeah. Daddy likes that," he pants, practically drooling over us. In the reflective surface behind Scarlett's head I can see the man adjust himself through his pants as he watches me make out with my girl. For someone who just called me a dyke a few minutes ago, he sure seems into this.

"You want to join us then, daddy?" Pulling away from Scarlett, I slink across the small space to the man.

My fingers lightly brush the stiffening cock through his pants before running up his chest and to the back of his neck. I pull him down to me, letting him kiss me. His hands grasp my curves and pull me against him as he grinds and grunts against me. Before I can pull away, another body moves in behind me. Scarlett's much more delicate form joins in, her tongue licking up my neck. I can't help the pleasured sigh that escapes me, nor the roll of my hips searching for some type of friction in my core as they both work me over with their tongues.

And then the elevator dings and the doors slide open. We disentangle quickly and face the empty hallway. My hand finds Scarlett's once again as I lead them down the hallway to room 313.

"Undress. Both of you...slowly," he demands gruffly, slumping down into a blue patterned chair that faces the bed.

"Caught in a web, soon to be dead," the demon singsongs as he appraises the feast that's readily come to be consumed.

Slinking out of my floral sundress and letting it pool on the ground at my feet, his eyes rake over my curves. The purple bra and panties I'm wearing are also some of Scarlett's favorites. I can feel her eyes on me as well. The heat of both their gazes on me is enough to make me combust.

Moving to Scarlett, I let my fingers lightly skim the bare flesh of her arms. Reaching the straps of the dress and pull them down, exposing her tightened nipples. She lets out the sweetest little sigh as the cool air whispers across her sensitive skin. Yanking the dress down the rest of the way, I expose every inch of her beautiful body.

"Nothing underneath?" I let my finger flick her exposed nipple lightly. "Such a naughty girl, aren't you?"

She nods, biting her lower lip between her teeth. She knows what that does to me.

"On the bed, spread your legs, show me that pretty pussy," I growl at her as I unclasp my bra and let my tits bounce freely.

My sweet girly willingly obliges, laying on her back, her legs spread wide, giving me a perfect view of her weeping cunt. She's a delicious sight, one I will never get sick of admiring.

"Eat her fucking cunt, dyke."

Shit. I almost forgot this asshole was here.

"Yes, daddy," I croon in a fake as fuck timid little voice, flashing him a sweet smile over my shoulder before turning my attention back to the form on the bed. Crawling on top of her, I let my lips lightly skim the warm and pale flesh of her thighs. She squirms in anticipation as I settle myself right between her thighs. Dipping a single finger into her core, I skim her outer lips.

"So wet for me already, aren't you princess?"

"Yes," she moans as I let my finger lightly tease her throbbing clit. The slickened bud hardens as I draw tiny figure eights against it, just like my girl likes. I've spent the last several months exploring her and learning exactly how to drive her wild. We have an eternity together, but that doesn't mean I can't savor every moment.

"Eat her fucking cunt, already. Stop messing around." I whip my head around to see our victim pumping his thick cock. His pants are pulled down his thighs as he sits in the same blue hotel chair, his eyes fixated on my fingers as they play with my girl's pretty pussy.

I keep my eyes on him, letting him think that he's in control as I lean down. I stick out my tongue and slide it through Scarlett's slick folds. His eyes widen and his breath quickens as he watches me taste her. He pumps his thick, veiny member harder.

"Like that, daddy?" I ask as I lick her again. Scarlett moans, her hands moving to her own breasts as she flicks her needy nipples.

"Let me see you stick your tongue in her tight hole. I want to watch you really fuck her with that tongue. Make her come on your fucking face."

Repositioning myself, I grab onto the back of both of Scarlett's thighs, opening her wide for me. Our eyes meet and I can see her need swirling in her irises. *She's such a delicious fucking feast.* I line my lips up with her clit and suck the hardened bundle of nerves, flicking it with my tongue. She bucks her hips up into my face but I pull back before she can get too excited. She mewls and whines for me. It's sweet. I move lower, circling her tight hole with the tip of my tongue

"Fuck," she whines. The sounds of her panting breaths mixed with the slapping of skin from behind us are sinfully delectable.

I let my tongue push into her tight opening slowly, teasing her. She loves when I play and tease with her, working her up to where she can't take it anymore. I love it too. I love when she begs me to make her come. With each thrust of my tongue into her warmth, I go slightly deeper and deeper.

And then hands on my hips drag me back.

"You think that's good? Wait until I tear this pussy apart," he pants in my ear as he lines up his stiff cock with my opening. "You're never going to want cunt again." He thrusts into me in one swift motion, making me cry out in pain and pleasure.

He pulls out and shoves himself in, all the way to the hilt, again. He might be a complete asshole but his cock is pretty great. It's long and thick and hits just the right spot inside that makes pleasure ripple through my core. My tits bounce wildly as he fucks me harshly.

"Tell daddy how good his cock feels filling up your tight pussy," he demands between thrusts.

"So good daddy. You feel so good."

Such a nice cock. Too bad it'll be no use to anyone after tonight.

"You're a good little cock whore for your daddy,

aren't you?"

"Yes daddy. I want to be your good little whore!"

"Eat her out while I fuck you, dyke."

Don't have to tell me twice.

I dive back into my girl. My tongue dipping into her coffee and caramel sweetness. Each violent pounding blow of his hips brings my face further and further into Scarlett's tight hole. With each thrust my tongue dives deeper into her, caressing her inner walls desperately. She is fucking drenched. Her sweet slickness dampens my chin. The feeling of his rock solid cock hitting me in just the right spot, combined with her taste on my tongue is almost too much. Heat coils in my core. My princess is clearly enjoying herself too, her mewling moans fill the room as I feast on her pussy with fervor while mine gets pounded from behind.

"Don't you fucking come, whore." The man drilling into me from behind grunts at my girl. "Get over here bitch and get on your knees. Suck my balls while I fuck this tight fucking cunt. Once you two get me off, you can play with each other."

The smell of magnolias permeates the air. My girl is afraid. If it's him or me she's afraid of though, I can't tell. I glance up, making contact with Scarlett over top of her clean shaven mound. She nods once, ever so slightly. She might be nervous, but my love is ready. It is time for the real fun to begin.

"She's not your whore. She's my queen. And she kneels

for no man."

I release the barbs from my inner walls, letting the demon take control.

"Time to cry. Time to die," he sings as he breaks loose from my soul.

Horns sprout from my head, my eyes shift, my tongue lengthens, limbs stretching and pulling as the Hell beast within is unleashed. And most importantly, my teeth come out to play with our new friend.

"What the fuck?" he shrieks in horror behind me but I'm too in awe to turn and soak in his fear. I'm entranced with the way Scarlett looks at me. I would expect her to look at me with fear or horror. However, all I see on her face is love and awe. She looks at me like I'm the most beautiful and powerful creature she's ever seen. *My violent little love.*

My barbs pierce his stiff member, feasting on his flesh and fear. He screams and squirms, trying desperately to push me off, even as he comes. His warm blood and cum coat my inner walls and I can't help the moan of pleasure that escapes my mouth.

"Is he good, baby?" Scarlett asks beneath me.

A wicked idea crosses my mind as his blood begins to seep out of my tight pussy, and down my thick thighs.

"You want to feel?" I ask my girl with a smirk on my face.

She grins and nods. That's all the permission I need.

Dipping my fingers between my folds, I coat them in the

warm liquid pooling there. The thick, red warmth coats my middle and forefinger. Pulling them out, I bring them up to the light, letting her see the blood covering my hand. Then I shove the fingers inside her.

"Fuck!" she screams as I fuck her with the blood of our victim.

"You like that? You like being my vicious little demon whore?"

The man screams behind me as he comes again, his soul nearly completely emptied now. I'm so close to finishing as his essence leaks out of him and into me. But, I want us to come all together.

Leaning down, I flick my forked tongue over Scarlett's clit. I pinch the hardening nub between the two ends of my demon tongue. She tastes like coffee, caramel, and death. It's fucking exquisite. She writhes and squirms at my assault, her inner walls fluttering around my bloodied fingers. She's close. His cock twitches inside me as I suck him more. They're both so close. I want to be covered in both of their cum.

"Come for me," I demand as I suck and fuck them both.

They oblidge. He empties the last of his soul into me, covering my inner walls with his essence. Scarlett screams as her walls clench around me, her thighs clamping around my head. Their combined pleasure pushes me over the edge. I moan into Scarlett's cunt as wave after wave of pleasured ecstasy rips through me. My entire body is rocked with sweet ripples of rapture.

When I finally come down, I unclench and my barbs recede. His limp, drained body falls to the floor with a thump. I raise my head, taking in the satiated form of my girl. She's a vision. Her skin is pink and glistening with sweat; her raven hair splayed around her head like a dark halo. She's a fucking queen—my demon queen. I've waited an eternity for a woman and a love like this. And now that I have her, I plan to spend the rest of eternity with her. An eternity to please her. An eternity to laugh with her. An eternity to love her.

ACKNOWLEDGMENTS

This book is for all the girls who want to feel strong and powerful. You deserve to be raised up and celebrated for being you. Stay strong and fierce my babes!

Thank you to my Betas! Justine, Angie, Kaitlen, Chelsea, and Lena please know how very much I appreciate you and your helpful feedback. You guys have been supporters of Morgan and her story since the jump and your positivity gave me the support to keep going!

I have two people who have truly supported me every step of the way with this project and I owe them so much. Darma - you're a beautiful ray of sunshine and I'm so grateful for you. You seriously are amazing and I am so lucky to have found you. Your help, your support, your friendship, your suggestions…all of it! Jenna–girl I would be lost without you! Your creative genius is astounding. I do not know how you do it! My cover is beautiful amazingness thanks to you. I know this one was more work than the last and I need you to know how much I appreciate your dedication to making this book beautiful inside and out!

A huge shoutout goes out to my editor! Mara you're a dang saint! Thank you for going through my chaos with a fine toothed comb and making it pristine. You're my savior.

To my good girls gone rogue - you guys kick ass! Love

you babes!

Finally, to everyone who read this book I owe you such a huge thank you! If you read this please know that I appreciate you. Morgan and Scarlett's story was so important to me and I hope they impacted you as much as they impacted me! Thank you lovely readers.

COMING EARLY 2025

Will

3 Months Prior

Tonight was a colossal fucking mess. A shiver creeps up my spine as I think of *her...it...*whatever the fuck that was. I keep telling myself it must have been some fucking trick or some shit. Girls don't grow horns. It must have been some type of costume shit.

Then why is Kyle dead? His corpse left rotting in a damn pumpkin patch.

Fuck. I have no fucking clue what happened tonight. Maybe it was a dick move to leave his girlfriend out there with that thing, but whatever I tried to get her to go. I sling back the remainder of the clear liquid in my glass, letting the alcohol burn its way to my core.

My phone! I recorded it all on my phone! There's fucking proof! This will sell just as well, if not better than some of my homemade passed-out-chick-gets-gang-banged videos. People will eat up a video of a sweet seductress turned demon right in front of their eyes!

Shoving my hand into my right pocket where I usually keep my phone, I come up empty. Shit! I put my hand into my left pocket to be met with nothing but fabric. Shit! Where the fuck did it go? I had it in my hand, I was filming, and then…I'm not sure what happened. I must have dropped it in the field. Shit! Maybe if I go back I will be able to find it and grab it. But then I will be at the scene of the crime if anyone shows up and finds Kyle's body. Might be too fucking risky. I should probably stay here, tucked safely in my casino, far away from whatever that shit was. Maybe I can get the video off the Cloud or some shit.

A flash of something pink catches my eye. There's usually not a lot of pink in this bar. It's a small casino bar. A handful of high top tables liter the front of the room with a large black bar taking up the entire back wall. A row of televisions playing various games sits above the underlit liquor bottles behind the bar. The patrons here are usually elderly slot machine addicts, or men looking to place a wager on a game. That's my normal job here—running the betting books. The hotel rooms upstairs allow me to conduct my other business venture out of the casino as well. Although, finding young and unsuspecting girls that my viewers would want to see drugged and fucked on live stream is not always easy hunting here.

But there's a sweet little thing right across the bar that would be perfect. She's lean but curvaceous with a tight ass. Her tanned skin is exposed in a short, little black crop top and black skirt. Her style is a bit alternative for my normal taste, but she's hot enough that it doesn't matter. What really sticks out about her though, is her hair—shockingly vibrant hot pink curls frame her sweet face.

I want her.

She has an arm slung over the back of the chair of one of my newer regulars. He's definitely an addict. He's lost more on games in the last few weeks than I'm sure he's made at whatever crappy day job he has in years. He's one of my new favorite customers. She's too young and too pretty for him though. He must be related to her in some way, I doubt they're together.

Trailing my fingers down my shirt, I try to decrease some of the wrinkles. I run my hand through my hair, pulling it out of my face.

As I approach them I hear the older man speak to her. "Liv, sweetheart, you don't have to worry about me. Weren't you and Celeste supposed to go out tonight anyway? Go! Be young and reckless and enjoy yourself."

"Dad, you know I'm happy to come hang out with you, always. Plus, Celeste never texted me back. She must be staying at school late tonight or something."

Just as I'm about to slide in front of them and make my move, a long and lean figure glides across the room to the girl. Erika. What is she up to?

Erika is a bitch—a crazy fucking bitch. But she is hot. Her dad owns the entire casino and she practically lives here. She approaches the pink haired girl from behind, running her fingers up the new girl's arm. I wonder how my brightly haired girl's flesh would taste. Would this sweet little thing be sad and sweet or feisty and full of fight as she lay beneath me, taking my pain? Erika leans in, whispering to the girl. I can see her tense but nod at whatever is whispered into her ear.

Interesting.

Erika slides her fingers into my new obsessions hand, pulling her away from the bar. The girl puts on a fake smile and says something to the older man before allowing Erika to lead her away. Erika holds her head high, clearly excited by whatever she has in mind for this evening. Maybe she needs a hand with that sweet little thing? Stalking my prey, I follow the sway of their beautiful hips towards the elevators.

Tonight just got fun again.

ABOUT THE AUTHOR

LO Gold is an indie author of dark and smutty stories. She lives in a college town somewhere in the middle of the US. She lives with her wonderful husband, goofy and loveable dog, grumpy cat, and beautiful children. She has a whole secret life that she lives in the real world but at night she opens her laptop and writes stories of dark chaos. She loves to read as much as she loves to write and has been inspired by all the hard working, kick ass women who have come before her and paved the way for this genre!

FOLLOW LO GOLD

If you liked this story and want to follow along on her journey follow her on Instagram, TikTok, and Facebook!

Find LO Gold Here:

Instagram – logold_author

TikTok – logold_author

Facebook — LO Gold's Good Girls Reader Group

Made in United States
North Haven, CT
15 February 2025